ALEXANDRIA REBORN
Book II

The Alexandria Rising Chronicles

MARK WALLACE MAGUIRE

To the EIDSONS

[handwritten signature]

Alexandria Reborn
Book II of The Alexandria Rising Chronicles
Copyright 2017 by Mark Wallace Maguire
Published by Speckled Leaf Press
First Edition
Cover and jacket design by Mark Wallace Maguire
Author photograph by Adam Miller

Printed in the United States of America

ISBN: 1546922717

www.alexandriarising.com
www.alexandriarisingchronicles.com
www.markwallacemaguire.com

FROM THE AUTHOR

There are far too many people to thank here, not only for their encouragement with this book, but especially their enthusiasm for my first novel, "Alexandria Rising." Your reaction and enthusiasm was a catalyst in me writing this sequel at such a fast pace. I cannot list everyone here, but you know who you are.

Several individuals played a pivotal role in this book coming to life.

Adam Miller, a longtime friend and talented writer, provided relentless encouragement and, without him, I doubt this novel would have seen the light of day.

My wife, Jami, was very patient in hearing me out, brainstorming with me and, most significantly, providing her own insights to the narrative.

Whitney Betts, my grandfather Bob Wallace, affectionately called 'PopPop,' and my Uncle Bruce Wallace aided in proofreading. Beth Poirier provided insight regarding layout. Thank you to all of them.

As a last perfunctory note, if you haven't read "Alexandria Rising," the first book in the Alexandria Rising Chronicles, I do encourage you to read that prior to this tome. While this book can be read by itself, the plot, characters and allusions would make more sense by reading the books in order of publication.

If you wish for extra insight, please visit the website, www.alexandriarisingchronicles.com, which features an array of interactive features including an extended appendices.

Enjoy the journey.

This book is dedicated to my conspirator, accomplice, fellow seeker, lover and wife, Jami.

"If we dig precious things from the land,
we will invite disaster."
-Attributed to Hopi Mythology

There is shadow under this red rock,
(Come in under the shadow of this red rock),
And I will show you something different from either
Your shadow at morning striding behind you
Or your shadow at evening rising to meet you;
-T.S. Eliot, The Wasteland

PROLOGUE

Virginia
Mid-Summer's Day
1776

D awn was just waking, the first faint lines of silver on the horizon, casting the slightest tints of cerulean onto the trunks of the trees, the thick blades of summer grass and the minuscule bubbles of dew that lined their stalks.

The statesman took it all in from behind his desk. His chair a weary companion to his now-strained back. The empty tea cups sat about as milestones of his work. It was the end of the night. Finally. He had been up for two days, feeding himself on a diet of hot tea and tobacco sucked from the end of a tooth-bitten pipe. Had packed and emptied and stirred the bowl repeatedly and the smoke hung above him in his study. Hovering. Shiftless. Almost like a shroud.

He reached for the pipe again. Picked a few flakes of Virginia gold leaves that had fallen to the desk from the bowl and deliberately packed it. Grabbed a candle for flame. Tilted it to the pipe. Then heat. Crackling. A flash of red. A cinder. Smoke. Puffs emanated from the bowl, slow discharges to meet with their cousins in the cloud above his desk. Thick thunderclouds.

The statesman watched the light outside grow, now illuminating the rolling hills, their shoulders singed in the light. He smiled to himself. Even after these years, his travels, his work, his lovers and his newfound place in this young country, he could find simple joy in the land. Always the land bringing him back. Always the call of this land. His land.

He took another celebratory suck of smoke. Discharged a plume. The smoke joining the cloud above him, an unholy matrimony of freedom and celebration, the statesman mused. If those leaves that were green just a few months ago knew what they would be partaking in, even their stalks would shiver in celebration.

The statesman stood. Buttoned his shirt. Donned his requisite jacket he had hung on the chair. No need to wake the servants. No need to wake his wife. No need to even say farewell to Sally. They all knew where he was going and when he would be back.

He gently grabbed the parchment from his tiny desk. Tied a leather ribbon around it and slid it into a cylindrical case. He glanced around the room again. The last of the candles succumbing to their suffocating swamp of wax. The plate of leftover ham and cornbread, half-eaten laid haphazardly on a plate. And the stone. Still the stone. Sitting on the desk. Its colors shimmering, the blues, the silver, the séance-laced shadows dancing around it like a parade of phantoms. He placed his palm over it. Felt the now-familiar shiver sear down his spine. His very fingers felt like flint sparking in rain, a weird magic of fire and ice. His eyes opened wider and, looking out the windows, he could see each blade of grass on the hills. Could see the ones bent with wind. The ones that grew too fast in the spring and now leaned at harsh angles, like hanged men, limp and useless. The ones that were growing late, but strong. Tiny shoots seeking sunlight. Then he lowered his hand, grasped the stone and, quickly, placed it into a thick leaden case which he closed, locked with a key that he tucked inside his jacket. A deep breath. A bead of sweat.

He shook his head. Flared his nostrils. Buttoned his coat. Ran a hand through his hair. Knew he could find a room in Philadelphia to tidy up. Ignored his ink-stained shirt, and half stubble on his face. Clinched his pipe in his mouth, the case under his right arm.

Then across the room. Closed the door softly behind him. Locked it. Walked on cat's feet to the front door, opened it and into the morning air.

The carriage was out front. John sat atop it. Waiting. Early as usual, a trait the statesman always admired.

"Good morning, sir. How are you this fine morning?" The words heavy and deep rolling out of the black man's mouth.

"I am fine, John. I am fine. Though not much sleep these past few nights. A big few days coming up and I've been at it all night writing again."

"Always writing, sir. If half of what the rumors say are true, that hard work is going to change everything. Will you be riding up top today, sir, or inside?"

"If you will excuse me, even though it is a lovely day, I think I will ride inside the carriage today. It is bound to be a long week and I'll need my rest however I can find it."

"Of course, of course. If you need anything, just let me know, Mr. Jefferson."

"I will John. I will. And, please, for the thousandth time, just call me Thomas."

He heard the low chuckle of the carriage driver above him as he climbed into the carriage. While he knew his worth, his place at this juncture in history, he did not want to stand on name and title and prestige – false or true – in any form. That would be a contradiction to the very words he had written.

"All set, Mr., I mean, Thomas?" The voice called.

"All set. Straight ahead. No need for any stops. No time for social visits or to check my vines," and then under his breath, "as much as I would love to."

The carriage set down the road, small skittles of pebbles churning underneath the wooden wheels. Inside the statesman was starting to fade, 3 days without sleep, catching up with him. But he was content. The sun was now rising strongly in the east, the full breadth of Monticello coming into view and under his arm he held the draft for the Declaration of Independence.

CHAPTER ONE

There was no wind. No smell of crunched leaves. Or damp earth.
A faint smell of pine. Or was it wood varnish? Minwax? Flashing images of pinewood derby cars, of glossy wooden canes in his grandfather's study.

Around him was a rigid silence.

He lifted his right eyelid. The weight heavy. But he had to wake up. He felt he had been so close the last few times. Before. Before the heavy lure of sedation and exhaustion lured him back in under. Under. Had it been hours? Days? Weeks? When was the last time he was awake, aware?

He was in a bed. He knew that, could feel a hard mattress beneath him. He stared up. Rand could decipher white pine logs through the dim light, the riddle of wood. Symmetrical, yet unique with their random brown knots. The glossy sheen reflecting faintly, a reassuring memory to the unthreatening signs of relaxation and comfort. Of mountain cabins in the North Georgia mountains he had visited as a child.

He turned his head. To the left. Slowly. His neck felt heavy, unused. Like a weight was pulling on it. He was met with the sight of a wall the color of firs and rich undergrowth in the forest. No windows. No pictures.

He slowly swiveled his head to the right. The spindly metal column of an IV stand greeted him. A half-filled IV bag hung from one of its arms. Rand's eyes followed its tube to where it wound its way under the sheets. Wriggled his fingers. Ah, there it was, neatly inserted into the top of his hand, the unnatural piercing and strange funnel of plastic and liquid into a vein. Heard a beep. Glanced up. Above the bag hung a plastic monitor. Saw the ubiquitous blinking green lights. Squinted. Could not decipher the digital numbers on its face.

A nightstand was wedged behind the IV stand. A table lamp aimed a pale yellow cone to the ceiling.

He peered around the remainder of the room. Nothing on the walls. No closet. No dresser. No desk. A half-open door was at the end of the room, but Rand could not distinguish what was beyond it, just a hint of light from what he imagined was a hall.

He inhaled deeply. Again, felt the immense drowsiness. Tremendous gravity on his forehead bearing down. He clenched his fists, the right one still tight with the IV running into it. The left one stiff, but working. Began seeking other injuries by slowly flexing and relaxing the rest of his upper body. Then a stinging. A small bite of white pain in his right shoulder. He remembered it. Yes, the pinch in his shoulder. He craned his neck. Saw a bandage. Yes, the bandage. Things began coming back. A gunshot? Was there a gunshot?

He stopped moving. Focused on the ceiling. Another deep breath. Sucked in his stomach. Nothing but the pinch from the tape on his shoulder stretching. Then flexed his legs. A hollow pain in his left thigh. He reached his left arm down, ran his hand over where it hurt. Felt a thick bandage, wrapping his whole thigh. What had happened there?

Rapidly blinked. Where was he? How had he gotten here? Then, he felt his eyelids beginning to droop, the warm lure of rest calling him.

"No," he groaned.

He was surprised at the croak in his own throat. The rasp. He cleared his throat, tried to speak again.

"Wake up. Wake up," his voice stronger now, but weak, and he coughed. The movement wracked his body and his shoulder gave a brief flare. He tried to stifle the cough, but it just made it worse and it sounded like cannons in the barren room.

A voice pierced through the cacophony.

"Rand? Rand? Are you awake?" A female's voice. Familiar?

He turned his head to see a silhouette at the door. It began moving toward him.

"Rand? Are you awake?"

He squinted. A blurry figure, then the face came into view, the small lamp casting odd shadows on the pert nose and thick lips in the half-light.

Hope Lightfoot.

"Hey," he managed, through a fit of coughing, "water?"

"Sure," she said, reaching down by the side of the bed. She lifted a cup of water. Held it to his lips. He drank deeply, felt the rivulets drip down his beard onto his bare chest. Didn't care. So thirsty.

"Okay, okay, that's enough, Rand. Just a little at a time."

"Hope?"

"Yeah, it's me. And you're finally up, sleepyhead."

A faint smile.

He grinned back. Weakly.

"What happened? Where are we?"

CHAPTER TWO

"You need to rest Rand," she guided her hand through his hair, tenderly. "Just go back to sleep. You need to heal up."

"No," another cough, "I don't. I've been asleep. Forever, it seems like. Where am I?"

She sighed.

"We're in a secure location about ten miles outside of a town you probably have never heard of – Mentone, Alabama."

"Mentone, Alabama? I've heard of Menlo, Georgia. Went camping near there once, I think. But, Mentone? What are we doing here?"

"This is one of our safe houses in North America."

"But, why here? Why Alabama?"

"Where is the last place you would look for us to be? People get this idea in their heads of clandestine work being done in New York, London, D.C. or Paris, but think about it, if you really want to get things done you want to be stationed in an out-of-the-way place. Here we're in the mountains, we have great canopy cover and we're secluded. The town of Mentone is about 15 minutes away and has a population of under 400. We're not only in the mountains of northwest Alabama, but most of this location is underground, like where we are now. Up top, as we call it, is a nice typical mountain cabin. Something you can rent on an Internet site."

Rand stared at her face. Waited for a moment of clarity. Something to reveal itself. Blank.

"But, how did I get here? How did we get here? The last thing I remember was lying in some type of a hospital bed, watching the news about a meteorite in Austria. What a joke it was. What a farce. Then you telling me," and here, pin needles raised on his neck, "that, that, there were more of…them…The Organization. That is the last thing I remember, the last time I think I was awake. Then just beds and…surgeries? Countdowns? Oxygen masks? Shots? Did we fly in an airplane? I don't know…everything has been a blur…weeks of dreams."

"We were in a hospital room in Berlin. But only briefly. We had taken a helicopter ride after the destruction of The Castle. I was okay, only nicks and bruises, but you had gunshot wounds and needed blood and surgeries. A shot to your right shoulder nicked off some of your clavicle that we had to scope out. Then there was the shot to your left thigh. Thank God that one went clean through."

Memories began flipping through his mind…white flashes… the bullet spiraling through the air…blood on his fist…Virgillius's blood…the cool handle of the gun in his hand…ear splitting explosions….a patch of blood blooming on Kent's shirt…the rock of the elevator…acrid smoke in his nostrils…blue flickering light…

"Are you okay?" Hope's words brought him back.

"Yeah, I guess. I guess. I just didn't think I would make it out of that. That place. Alive. I, I just did what I had to do. I never thought about after, you know? Like now."

"It's okay. You're safe. But, things have changed forever. I don't mean to be too blunt, but nothing will ever be the same for you."

CHAPTER THREE

A gentle knock on the door interrupted their conversation. Hope moved her hand away. Rand strained to see the face, but it was eclipsed by the dim light in the hall. Only a form. Then a voice. He knew the voice, but couldn't place it. Recognized the accent. German-tinged. Who was it? Who was it?

"Rand, good morning. How are you today? I am so happy to see you awake."

The figure entered the room, a squat body, white lab coat clinging to it like a shrunken cape. The face came into view. It was Dr. Dunkel. Dunkel from The Castle. The man with the oily smile, bright brown eyes and the penchant for Latin. Virgillius's assistant.

Rand began to panic. He yanked at the IV stand. Tried to lift it, but it was too top-heavy and awkward, rattling in its insistence to stay put. A hot twinge tore through his shoulder. Felt the cold medical tape straining and tearing the hairs out of his hand where the IV was. He glared at Hope. Looked for something, anything to use as a weapon. Reached for the lamp. Grabbed it. Tried to yank it out of the socket. Its cord stubbornly stayed plugged into the wall. Shit. The man was getting closer. His mouth moving, but Rand couldn't hear the words. Just a wall of static. Then there was shouting. Louder and louder.

"Rand! Rand! Stop! Stop!" Hope shouted.

"Hell no!"

"Rand!" Hope yelled again and grabbed his forearm, her fingers clamping down on a series of stitches he hadn't noticed. He flinched, but did not cease. The plug on the lamp had to give. Dunkel was stepping closer, soft padded feet.

"Rand! Stop! He's on our side. Listen, he's one of us."

Rand froze in motion. His hand still gripped the lamp. Knuckles white. His eyes flitting between Hope's impassive face and the smiling Dunkel who had stopped in his tracks and had his hands lifted in a non-threatening pose.

"Yes, Rand. Listen. She is telling the truth. I am, as she says, one of you. I have been helping take care of you."

Rand stared at him hard. Waited for the man to budge. Anything. Any sign. Something.

Hope's words split the tension.

"Rand, do you remember? Do you remember when I told you that I knew someone inside of Kent's circle who said they were going to kill you? The night I tried to get you out of there before you went back and blew everything to hell. Do you remember?"

Someone in the circle...Kent using him as a plaything...experiments...the knock on the door... smuggling him out to the roof where the helicopter waited, blades whirring...someone in the circle...yes, she said that. Someone wanted to save him.

"Yeah," Rand spoke softly. "I remember."

"This is him. This is the one who warned me. Who saved you. Who saved us. It was him. It is him."

Dunkel gave a slight bow. The toothy smile again.

"I am sorry for everything back there, Rand. But you are in a safe place and I have been watching you in your recovery. I... hope...I hope...we can be friends, perhaps," then as if reading Rand's expression, "or, if not friends, at least allies. I made a promise to your grandfather over 20 years ago. You were never to be involved with The Organization, the Slendoc Meridian, any of it. And, if you ever did become involved for any reason, I was to protect you. I swore my life on that promise. I never forgot it and have not forgotten it now. I kept up with you through the years, out of duty, but I had, I guess, forgive the expression, written you off. Then he died and then, God knows, when you came to that place, I knew things had to change. I had contact with these people," he nodded his head toward Hope, "But, you coming to

Austria sealed the deal as you might say. Imagine that, a promise from a prince among men made to a young scientist taking two decades to fulfill. Life is funny, isn't it?"

"Yeah, life is funny," Rand said, no filter on his sarcasm. "Sorry, Doc, but all of these damn coincidences just aren't very funny anymore, or amusing or serendipitous or however you want to put it. It's nice knowing you helped me out and knew my grand-father and all that - shit, everybody says they knew my grandfa-ther - but I'm done here. Done with you. Done with all this. I just want to go home. And that is what I plan to do right now."

The words in a panicked fury out of his mouth.   Despite the haze of medicine, he planted his hands on the bed, and ignoring the pain in his shoulder, began to push himself off the mattress.

"Rand," Hope began, her hand still on his arm, a quaver in her throat. Rand looked at her. She swallowed. Straightened her back. Her nostrils flared. The professorial look in her visage again. A look Rand had learned to love and hate during his time at The Castle. "Rand," she began again. "Rand. You can't go back home –"

"Okay. I am a little confused and, yeah, I may not be all the way awake. I need coffee, lots of it. But, I do know this. I am done. I don't need to wait. Why do I need time? When am I going back to Atlanta? I may not be 100 percent healed, but I am ready. I can recover just as well in my shack of a house with a book as I can here. I'm ready."

Hope's grip tightened on his arm, she stared at the floor. Then lifted her eyes to Rand. He thought he could detect a slight well-ing to them. A shimmer of wetness. Was she going to cry?

"Rand, you, you have no home anymore. You can't go back to Atlanta…you're dead. Out there, you're dead."

"What do you mean I'm dead?" Agitation edged his words. "I'm not dead. I'm right here. Kent," he inwardly shuddered at saying the man's name, but pressed on. "Kent said I – or whatever they said, a version of me – was in a hospital from a car wreck. I asked him to go ahead and finish that thing. To kill me off, to do it, but he said he wanted to wait, then –"

"Rand, listen, I –"

"No, you listen. I waited. I did," his voice rising, then sinking, "I did what I had to do" the memories flooded back now. Dark splotches of red splayed across the floor of The Cavern. His hand sore from backhanding Virgillius. Kent's kneecap buckling under the gunshot. Then the blaze of color and blue fire. A flash of pain seared across his head. All. Too much. The words burst from his mouth louder than he expected. "But, I did it. It was horrible, but damn it, I'm done. I'm done. I just want to go home."

Hope held her head erect, but there was sympathy in her eyes. And a sadness Rand had not seen before.

"Rand…you can't...you can't go home. Ever again. Kent had already killed you – or whatever version, person, whatever of you in the Atlanta hospital – when you were in The Castle. Before the dig even…He made the call to Atlanta. They had a funeral. The body they used was all mangled and burnt up. They only identified you from your driver's license they had stolen. You see, he never intended to keep you alive. You're dead now. And if you weren't, or your identity wasn't, you still can't go home. They surely have everything back there monitored. Your house or what was your house. Your grandmother's house. Your friends. I'm sorry. I really am….but, right now, we're all you have."

Rand sat silent. Staring at the wall. Dumbfounded. He could not believe it. This was supposed to be over. He made the sacrifices. He did the things he never wanted to do, never dreamed of doing. And, yet, he knew it was true. Hope's words made sense. Hell, they made perfect sense. He believed it in his head, but not in his heart. Too much. Too much.

"Rand. Will you be okay?"

"I, I don't know," he hung his head, clinched his eyes shut to push back the welling tears. "Can I just get some coffee and something to eat?"

CHAPTER FOUR

The grits swelled to the edges of the bowl, a thick slice of butter melting in its center. Two pieces of crisp bacon on a smaller plate. He cradled a cup of coffee in his hands.

"Remember Rand, eat slowly. You haven't had much to eat the last couple of weeks. We fed you light foods like yogurt and oatmeal. If you eat too much, too quick, it will not be pretty."

"I understand. Little bit by little bit. But, thanks for this breakfast. I love a Southern breakfast. All I need is a couple of biscuits and gravy and some eggs."

"All in good time," she said. "And grits? I don't know how you eat them."

"You don't know what you're missing. You can eat them with cheese, gravy, shrimp, sausage. Food for the body and soul," he said, lifting a spoonful.

"Well, like they say, Southern boy can survive…on anything apparently."

"It's country boy can survive, not Southern boy can survive. Don't confuse being Southern with being country. Hollywood stereotypes," he shook his head. "But, on the grits? Okay. Take your stereotype, you just don't know what you're missing out on, which is fine, more for me."

They were sitting at a table on the deck of the cabin, the typical Southern humidity dissipated in a breeze that blew wisps of clouds overhead. The cabin was perched on the side of a steep ridge and overlooked miles of gently sloped mountains covered in a hundred shades of green. Though he had never been to Northwest Alabama, Rand was familiar with the geography. The last Southern bits of the Appalachian Mountain range. The little brothers. Oh yes, these were mountains, but were rolling. More like shoulders, than knives. More grass underfoot and deciduous leaves overhead, than hard slate and evergreen. He knew the forests that covered these mountains. Lots of shadows in the underbrush, smell of earth, the hypnotic buzz of insects and gurgles of hundreds of streams and creeks that emptied into swelling rivers or lakes.

Rand drank deeply another cup of coffee. He had exchanged a ridiculous hospital gown for a pair of khaki cargo pants, a black T-shirt and hiking boots. He had also received an accessory forced upon him by Hope – an aluminum cane, "just until you get full strength," she promised.

They had left his room and taken wooden stairs up to the main floor where he was greeted with the signs typical to a mountain cabin. Small kitchen. Modest furniture. A few stuffed deer heads stared down at him from white pine wood walls. His thigh was still stiff and he bore a limp, but he was surprised at how little it actually hurt. Rigid? Yes. But the pain was far less hampering than even a sprained ankle he suffered years before playing football.

"Hope, how long was I out? Asleep in twilight or whatever you call it?"

"I don't know. Maybe two, three weeks? You underwent several surgeries. Then there were injections, grafting, artificial muscle replacement. They had you on the IV drip constantly. You've probably lost 15 pounds."

"Injections, grafting, muscle replacement?"

"Yes. We removed the bullet from your shoulder and extracted the bone fragments and we had to clean your leg wound, too. Then we did a series of gene replacement injections, insertions of new tissues, re-coupling of blood vessels. We tried to keep most of the replacement tissue and bone organic, but needed to take some synthetic measures as well to ensure that you healed quickly."

"Synthetic?"

"Yes. Part of your trapezius muscle in your shoulder is now –

well without getting into the scientific details – is basically made from a filament that resembles artificial fishing line."

"You got to be kidding me. Fishing line?"

"Believe it or not, the type of chemical in fishing line is excellent for replacing muscles. In many cases, the elasticity and strength is better than what was there before."

"But, but, who did all this? Isn't Dunkel a psychologist of sorts? And you? You don't have a medical background? Or do you?"

"No," she laughed. "No, not me or Dunkel. We had a team of surgeons flown in. They worked around the clock. Your last injection was probably two days ago, but with all the trauma your body has undergone, we've kept you sedated for rest if nothing else. Of course, we also had special fluids and electronic pulses used to keep your muscles from atrophying."

"So, I'm like the Million Dollar Man, now?"

"No, not quite. But you are healing very quickly. Usually, it can take 3 to 6 months for a bullet wound to repair itself, especially if broken bone is involved like your shoulder. But, you should be close to typical within a week."

He shook his head, scooping another bite of grits out of the bowl, pausing for a moment to appreciate their odd little orbs shimmering in the sunlight.

"Gunshots. Surgery. Grafts. Injections. And then I was unconscious for weeks. Well, that explains why I'm so hungry."

"Well, enjoy it. If you're up for it after those grits, we can get to work."

"Work? Are you kidding me? I just saved the planet and you want me to work? I need at least six weeks of vacation, minimum," he winked at her as he lifted the coffee cup to his lips.

She sighed, but there was a hint of a smile.

"So, this is it?" She asked.

"This is what?"

"This is you...you when you aren't under watch or being guarded or back there. This is you, full of yourself?"

"Oh, I guess so. I am who I am. But right now I am just trying to get a laugh somewhere. Anywhere. Anything to give my mind a break."

She nodded, eyes downcast.

Then, in an exaggerated Southern gentleman accent, added, "Ain't that right, sugar pie?"

He finally got the smile he wanted. Damn she was beautiful. He had known it since he first saw her, knew it all along. But, seeing her here, the green mountains behind her, the breeze twisting her hair that hung along her smooth neck, the absence of strain in her eyes, on her brow, her lips. This was different. He must have stared too long.

"What are you thinking about Rand?"

"You."

Most women would have blushed, Rand knew. A demure nod, a smile. But, Hope was not most women. He remembered that when she replied.

"Okay, enough, Romeo. Save your charm for later. I know you have questions and knowing you, probably a list a mile long."

He shrugged off the sting.

"Okay, then. Later. But, this place. Tell me more about this place before we, 'get to work.' We're in a mountain cabin. I got that. I know there is a basement of sorts where my bed is. I guess there are other rooms. What else do I need to know?"

Her body relaxed in the seat. Her hands clasped in front of her lap. Professorial. Erect.

"Like I said, this is all a cover. From the road or above, just a quaint mountain cabin. We're on a cul de sac. A place to retire or rent. Two stories. A couple of decks and a fire pit in the yard. We also keep an old SUV out front we drive into town a couple of times a week for groceries, mail and supplies. We only go two at a time in case the locals get nosy or a chance satellite sweep from The Organization notes any anomalies, like eight people living in a mountain cabin. The house and car are registered in the name of a semi-retired insurance executive and his wife from Omaha. Others of us, if we're seen with him, are relatives. Two people actually live up here full-time, Shane and Amy Sheffield. They're out buying groceries right now. Great folks. Loads of laughs. And, yes, your room is part of the basement where we have our living quarters. It is nothing spectacular. Spartan, but it works. Beneath that is another level."

"Another level? You people really like underground stuff. How did it all get – well, made – without anyone noticing?"

"The other level is significantly large and houses a few rooms, including our communications center and a medical center where you spent most of your first week here until we moved you to a private room. And how did this get built? Well, construction on this site began in the 1970s. There was a lone farm here run by a widower and three kids. We bought it from him. Then, we took our time to construct it the way we wanted to. Brought in construction crews from Huntsville and Chattanooga. Told them it was a government-related project. Paid them well. Kept everything hush-hush. I am sure there are more details to it than that, but that is the gist of it."

"Okay. I think I've had enough coffee now, so I've got to ask you the million dollar question: Who is we?"

"We're…well, it's rather a long story, but we're, we're the ones who split. Who left The Organization when things began to stray off course, to change from the original purpose."

"Okay, but, what do you do? I mean, what is the mission, the purpose? Do you just try to destroy The Organization?"

"No and yes and no. It's complicated."

"Try me."

Hope exhaled heavily. "Rand, I'm really not the person who you need to talk to about all of this. There are others that can explain it better. But, our people, our group split from The Organization because the use of the Slendoc Meridian had become corrupt. It had become more about power and weaponry and technology. We used to be good stewards at creating and developing new medicines, technologies, governments and art. It was not only artists like Shakespeare and Monet who used it, but visionaries in government and society like Thomas Jefferson. But, the original intent was corroded. Had been for decades. And our purpose is to stop them. To destroy them before they destroy this world as we know it."

"But, what about the Slendoc Meridian itself? Do you try to destroy it, too?"

"For a long time we tried to keep it, well, safe. But now we learned it's better to destroy it, than to be destroyed by it."

"So, they're happy with me destroying the stash in Austria?"

.

"Yes. I mean, it – well you – came out of left field, but, yes, when you boil it down they are pleased. Everything is just complicated."

"Trust me, I know about complicated. What do you think the last few weeks have been for me? You want to try a little harder than just saying complicated?"

"Rand, there are others who can explain it better than me. Others you will be meeting soon, I promise. All I can say now is we're the ones who are doing the right thing, making the right choices. You've got to trust me."

Rand looked around. He had been told his body was healing. Had been half-lulled into a trust. And yet, he could still not be sure. The last sips of coffee puddling at the bottom of his cup. Fast moving clouds throwing shades and shadows across the mountains.

"Trust you?" he scoffed. "What other choice do I have?"

The comfort of the sun and the breeze waned with his words. He looked at Hope. A blue cast over her face now, the shadow of a cloud drifting overhead.

CHAPTER FIVE

"**N**o more elevators," Rand sighed. "I mean, I really have come to hate elevators."

"Don't be a baby. This only goes down to the level beneath this. It was installed in the mid-80s when they needed to bring in larger equipment like those huge early computers, and other, technologies. We do have stairs too, but with your leg, I figured this would be easier."

They were at the end of the hall in the basement. Had passed his open bedroom door. The IV still waiting. The desk lamp still on. He saw two more doors across from his room, both closed. Somewhere he heard a shower running, a murmur of voices.

Now, they were waiting on the elevator. The doors slid open. Rand was greeted by a faded brass interior and what resembled a brick floor.

"This is really old, isn't it?"

"Yes. They haven't updated it in years. But it still works and that is all that matters. You'll find with us, we don't stand on pomp and circumstance."

The doors closed, a loud clank. The smell of an old office building. Even traces of cigarette smoke lingered in the elevator.

Another clank. A motor. Then descent.

The elevator door slid open to reveal a wide eggshell-colored hall with a series of unmarked doors on each side. A line of fluorescent light fixtures threw stark shadows on the walls. Oddly, the hall ended with a bright blue door proclaiming, 'Bathroom' in bright white letters.

Hope stepped out first, Rand behind her tentatively, glancing to his right and left. His guard still up.

"Door number one, door number two or the bathroom, what shall the choice be Miss?"

She shook her head.

"I swear if I would've known you would have woken with this much gusto, I would have requested a stronger sedative in your drip."

"All bull aside, Hope. I am happy just to be alive."

"I know. I know."

And then, finally, she reached back and grabbed his hand in a tight squeeze. She drew him close behind her. He nuzzled into her hair. Buried his eyes, his nose, his mouth against her neck. Heard a soft groan escape her lips. He began to wrap his other hand around her, to touch her, to pull her close, then -

"Hey! And just on time!" A nasal voice broke the moment.

The door to the immediate right swung open and a wiry man in his mid-20s greeted him. Tight cropped black hair. Brown eyes. Raven tattoo on his neck. White T-shirt with a photo of Jimi Hendrix sketched on it. Rand stiffened. Quick formality. Emotions guarded.

"So we finally got him here! The star of the show! The man who brought down The Castle," he said.

"Nothing more than a Castle Made of Sand," Rand said, referring to the T-Shirt.

The reference was lost on the man, who pushed by Hope and extended a pale hand to Rand, who, on instinct, shook it, its translucent flesh tender and limp under his own grip. If the oddness of the handshake bothered the man, it didn't register on his face.

"Rand, Rand, Rand. That's all I've been hearing about since you got here, bro! And here you are in the flesh. I'm Declan."

"It's a pleasure to meet you Declan," Rand said, though he wasn't sure if using the word pleasure would be considered lying.

Declan gave Rand the up and down look, stared into his eyes, looked again at his chest, his arms.

"You need something?" Rand asked, half annoyed by the examination.

"No, no bro. You're good. I was just expecting someone, you know, stronger, taller, like with a superhero build. More muscular, like a bad-ass. But, you're good. Come on in guys."

"Glad to know I'm good," Rand muttered.

Rand and Hope entered a room that appeared transported out of Silicon Valley. Sleek ergonomic desks jutted from the walls. Monitors hung from the ceilings, code and data streaming across their flat surfaces. Cold blue and blinking green lights emanating from everywhere. The smell of machinery was in the cool air and the only sounds were the whirring of electric fans and the hum of an air conditioner unit. In the center of the room, surrounded by a phalanx of towering computer terminals, was a raised desk that gave the impression of a dais.

"So, what do you think? Impressed, bro?" Declan didn't wait for an answer. "This is the setup of all setups. It's like the Matrix in here. Only I'm the Matrix."

"Yeah, sure," Rand said, who though not a Luddite, had never considered computer technology to be one of humankind's greatest inventions.

Beside him, Hope shivered.

"You okay?" He asked.

"Yeah, just cold. We have to keep it cold in here for the computers. I need a sweater every time I come down here."

"Hey Doctor, we got to do what we can do to keep the Anulap alive."

"Anulap?" Asked Rand. "What is that an acronym for?"

"Not an acronym bro." Declan raised his eyebrows, a tinge of condescension in his eyes.

"That's what he calls it, or calls this," Hope said motioning to the fixtures throughout the room. "Anulap. Named after the Polynesian God of Wisdom."

"Hmm...that's a bit brash isn't it?" Rand commented.

"Bro, not brash at all. This is what keeps us up on the East Coast. I named her Anulap because she is wisdom. She runs the wheels within wheels. The queen of codes, the goddess of algorithms. Our well of information."

"Well, don't confuse information with wisdom," Rand said.

Declan shot him a quizzical look. Then an empty laugh.

"Okay, bro. I gotcha. Philosopher, huh? The warrior philosopher king thing. I get it. Cool."

"Who helps you run all of this?" Rand asked.

"Just me, my man. Just me. I keep trying to get Hope to come down here and spend an evening with me, but she's not taken me up on it yet," a leering grin on the face. "But, that's cool, she'll come around."

A quick stab of jealousy jolted Rand. Then was gone. He had nothing to fear from this guy. Had to tell himself that again, though.

"Anyway, Rand, until I get some company it's just me and Anulap. We've got a good relationship. We take care of each other," Declan said.

"Okay. Sounds good, then." Rand was intrigued and, for some reason, slightly repulsed by this man. Declan still smiling as if waiting for another question or a compliment, hands on his narrow hips. Smile transfixed. There was a trace of overcompensation. Rand knew he was one of those guys you knew loved practicing who they were in front of a mirror.

"Okay then," Rand replied.

"Okay, bro, I'll see you soon."

"Okay, boys," Hope interjected. "Let's go Rand, I'll give you the rest of the tour."

Hope turned to leave. Rand went to shake Declan's hand. He was offered a fist bump instead. Rand didn't bump fists, so he leaned back on his old habits and grabbed the man's fist and shook it vigorously. For some reason, Rand always amused himself by doing it. A look of confusion erased the cocky smile that was affixed to Declan's face.

"Nice to meet you, Declan. I'll be back down later."

"Catch you later, bro. And you too, Doctor-Light-Up-My-Night."

CHAPTER SIX

"What the hell was that? Doctor Light-Up-My-Night? Come down and visit me?"

"Rand, relax," Hope said, laying her hand on his arm. "He's harmless."

The two of them alone in the hall. One hand on his cane, his other clinched in a fist.

"Still, I don't like it...I mean, we're together, you and me, aren't we?"

"Yes, I mean, I guess so, as much as being together can mean in the last couple of weeks."

"But, doesn't he know that? I mean, come on."

"Rand, everybody on our side doesn't know everything. I filed my report. They had briefings from Dunkel, but I didn't go into all of our...details. That's our business."

"And what exactly is the nature of our business as you call it?" He struggled to keep any anger out of his voice.

"Can we just talk about this later," a bit of irritation.

"Sure, sure..." The wind out of his sails, a moment's buoy-ness eclipsed by a shadow of doubt. "Well...what's next?"

"Perhaps the most important thing in the building."

He followed to the end of the hall to the door marked, "Bath-room."

"Ah, finally showing a sense of humor, Doctor, I like to see it. In many ways, it is the most important part of the building."

She rolled her eyes at him.

"You rolled your eyes at me! Literally, you just rolled your eyes. I can't believe this," humor edged his voice.

She shook her head, a lock of her black hair falling over her cheek, where he thought he detected a glimmer of a smile.

"Follow me," she said as she fished a key out of her pocket and inserted it into the lock.

Rand stepped into a rough-hewn room. Above, a string of yellow bulbs lit a narrow passage. Beneath his feet was slate gray rock. To his left, six backpacks hung on hooks. He could see the outline of what appeared to be an automobile squeezed into the tunnel. The air was damp, his skin already clammy.

"More tricks? What? Secret passages?"

"This Rand is our escape route. If anything ever happens, come here immediately. Take the car. This tunnel descends about 300 feet in less than a quarter of a mile. At the bottom of this tunnel is a door that opens onto a gravel road. Turn right. You'll go about two miles and then it empties onto a highway. You have a modified satellite phone in your backpack. Turn it on and press 33."

"Whoa, whoa, slow down, slow down. How am I supposed to remember all of this? Is this written somewhere or what?"

Hope stared at him. Almost sternly.

"Rand O'Neal," a scold. "How are you supposed to remember this? I am baffled. You memorize it. You should know that. Don't make this harder than it is. Why would we write anything down? We don't want records, don't you understand?"

"Okay, okay, okay. You're just going a little fast."

"Well, catch up then. This is important. In addition to your satellite phone, each pack also contains a passport, a Glock with eight magazines, a Taser and a full-sized straight edge K-Bar. There is also $1,000 in cash in multiple currencies."

"Taser? Glock? Passports too? How did you even get my picture?"

"Rand, come on. You've got your face in tons of places. Your driver's license, real passport, even those silly photos your old job put of you on the website last year when you won that award. We just found them, edited and then your new buddy Declan made them. Everything is legit."

"So, do I just grab a bag and hope I get the right one? How am I supposed to keep up?"

"It's simple. You're green."

Rand studied the bags again. Noticed each one had a tag at the top. A spectrum of colors. Purple. Red. Yellow. Blue. Brown. And green.

"And, wait a second, you said if anything happens, open the bathroom door, grab my pack and escape in the car?"

"That's right."

"What about the car? I assume it's an Aston Martin?"

"Oh, so you're James Bond now. And what does that make me, Pussy Galore?"

"I certainly hope so," he said.

She pulled a penlight out of her pocket. Switched it on. Then there it was. In all of its non-glory. It was probably four decades old and once had been a navy blue. But now was covered in pollen and a morass of dead leaves on its hood and roof, and it appeared a dull, sickly green in the light. It was a 1984 Chevrolet Cavalier station wagon.

"This?" Rand asked. "You've got to be kidding me. I'll be lucky to get galore of anything driving this heap."

"Settle down. Remember, what you see isn't always what you get."

"I surely hope so."

"Okay, let me put it this way. I'm not well-versed in car talk, but Shane had a V8 engine installed. That's a lot of power, right?"

"Sure, that's good, but what the about the glass? Bulletproof? Does it come with any other accessories? Smokescreen? Eject seats?"

"No. The keys are in the ignition. Oh, and, speaking of," then reaching into her pocket, she withdrew a key she handed to him. "And now you have your key to this room. Any questions?"

"No, I guess not. Just quite a bit to take in."

"I can imagine. Now, you need to rest for a couple of hours. I've got some work to do with Dunkel, then I want you to go spend some time this afternoon with Declan before dinner."

"Well, that's just perfect, because Declan is exactly the one person I want to spend time with now that I'm back among the living."

CHAPTER SEVEN

He was back in his room. Alone. The door shut behind him. Unlocked. The IV drip gone. Lying on his bed. Staring at the ceiling. The riddle of knots. A stack of books was waiting on his nightstand when he returned. Rand picked them up, eyed each one.

"U.S. Army Survival Guide."

"Guide de espionage: Secret Secteur, 1873."

"The Art of War. Sun Tzu."

"The Secret Agent: By Joseph Conrad."

"The best of Ian Fleming."

He wanted to nap, still felt sluggish after all the time he had been under, the caffeine wearing off. But, his mind wouldn't switch off. Too many questions. Too much angst. He knew he needed sleep. Closed his eyes. Tried to quell any anxiety. Breathe in. Breathe out. He was on the cliff of consciousness segueing into dreams when there was a knock at the door.

"Come in," Rand said.

Hope opened the door, came in, shut it behind her.

"Sorry to wake you."

"That's okay, I wasn't asleep anyway," he lied.

"I see you got your reading material?"

"Yep. This is interesting stuff," he said, pulling himself to a sitting position. "And I see the value in some of this, like the army survival book, this French spy guide, but why the fiction? I don't quite get it."

"You know our friend, Ian Fleming, right? The James Bond author?"

"Of course, I do Miss Moneypenny," Rand offered his best Sean Connery impersonation.

Hope shook her head in amusement, "Nice try, but, that sounds more like Jimmy Stewart. Fleming was a spy before he was an author. People forget that. Some of the best fiction books written have excellent methods for espionage, shifting identities, creating illusions and so forth. While that army guidebook might save your life in a jungle dying from thirst, the creativity of a good fiction writer might save your life in a city being pursued by people."

"So, to what pleasure do I owe this visit? I thought you said you had work to do and for me to rest before meeting with Declan."

"Well, we had something come up from Anulap and I need to go into town to post some letters."

"Post letters?"

"Yes. Letters. Postcards. When it comes to communication, we try as much as possible to stay off the grid. Sometimes, we'll use a HAM radio with ciphers and codes. The list goes on."

"But, what about when you do go out in public? To post letters or whatever. How do you avoid detection? Cameras are everywhere. The Organization's ability to tap in to anything, anytime."

"That's another reason we're in Mentone, not exactly cutting-edge surveillance technology. When we do go into more populated areas, it is still not as daunting as you might think. First of all, too many choices can mean no choices, right? They may have access to thousands of cameras and other monitoring devices, but if you don't know where to look, or more specifically, what you're looking for, well, then you're just tossing darts in the dark. Even with all that, I still wear a disguise. Nothing too intense, but you might be surprised at how much you can get away with a wig, some make-up and a glasses."

"I'll be damned. Disguises. Well, I always did want to play dress up. You know Halloween was one of my favorite holidays. Back in college, one year –"

"Rand," she cut him off. "Save the stories for another time. I don't mean to be rude. But the truck is leaving and I've got to –"

"Go post your letters."

"Trust me," she said, her arm laying lightly on his, "We'll have plenty of time to catch up later. But, since you're awake, how about you go ahead and go down and meet with Declan."

He nodded. As much as he dropped his iron walls for her, she always found a way to slip in a gust of cold wind.

"See you in a little bit," she leaned over and gave him a peck on the forehead.

A peck on the forehead? What the hell was that? He watched her saunter out of the room, his eyes strained in the lingering scent of her fading perfume.

CHAPTER EIGHT

"**D**uder! You made it!" Declan rose behind his desk and stood up, stretching.

"Yes, sir." Rand said.

"Looking good my man. Where's the cane?"

"I left it."

The wound still ached and Rand was shuffling, rather than walking, but he didn't want the cane. Had eyed it. But, abandoned it leaning on his bed. Once you go forward. Never go backwards. Another one of his grandfather's sayings.

"Wow, they got you on some of that good stuff huh? Superman shit. Already healing up like Luke Skywalker in a Bacta tank." Declan smiled, proud of his own joke.

"A Bacta tank? Skywalker? I don't know about that, but the only canes I like are the ones that have secret compartments for whiskey or swords. This one had neither so…anyway, here I am."

"Cool. Come on up to my command center."

Rand walked up a small ramp that led to the raised desk overseeing the room. An empty chair welcomed him, shiny silver, almost glowing in the low light. Rand sat. Felt the cool aluminum sticking to his palms. The desk held an array of relics from last century and today. Two die-cast bulky walkie-talkies. A variety of tools. Half-taken apart hard drives. And clumps of wires. All lorded over by two monitors that stood in the middle of the desk, screen-savers from 'The Matrix' scrolling.

"Comfy?" Declan asked.

Rand nodded.

"Okay, then, scoot on up here beside me so you can get the better view. Right on. Well, how much do you know about digital communications?"

"Not a lot. I mean, I know enough to keep myself alive," Rand thought of the iPhone trade he had made in the Shannon Airport bathroom. His plan of misdirection. Misinformation. It had worked. Then, he recalled the face of Billy Gallagher staring back at him from the newspaper clipping. The washed out smile. The blurred words. A simple trade that resulted in murder. He shivered.

"You okay, dude?" Declan interrupted his thoughts. "You aren't cold natured like the good doctor are you?"

"I'm fine. I'm fine…Okay on technology," Rand cleared his throat. "Well, I know enough about phone tracking, GPS, tracing phone calls, all that. Nothing too fancy. Just to make sure that if you go anywhere to not take anything that can be tracked…"

"Good start, dude. Good start. A lot of people know that and a lot of people don't, you know? People, bro. They just get like addicted to their phones and their cars and their ATM cards and don't even think about what kind of trail they're leaving, so, anyway when we communicate we mainly use old ways. Like postcards –"

"Letters," Rand interrupted. "HAM radios, codes, Old World tactics like that, right? Hope told me."

"Okay, okay," Declan raised his hands slightly as if offended. "Cool, bro. But if we really need to communicate digitally. Like, if it is extra important, and we can't wait for FedEx or the postman, then we use a digital chain. A super long chain. False email addresses that link to false email addresses that link to defunct phone numbers in the Third World. Then we match that up with extra-terrestrial communications."

"What? Extra-terrestrial? Aliens? You've got to me kidding me."

A smile encompassed the face. A cocky laugh: "Yes, extra-terrestrial. As in not on earth. Satellites. I suppose I could have just said 'satellites,' but I like the phrase and, technically it is correct."

Rand didn't find the humor in it. Poor word play. It reminded him of an egotistical reporter at the newspaper who made remarks like, "What do Canadians call Thanksgiving? Thursday." Rand enjoyed wit and word play, but held masters of the obvious in thin regard.

"Satellites," he exhaled. "Okay."

"Yep. There are like 2,000 satellites in orbit right now around the earth. We can send dead links, convoluted links and more to these. We can even land small transistor codes on space junk. Imagine this. We terra link to like 20 locations mainly in Africa and Eastern Russia where communications are very slow and prone to occasional black outs. Then we run those signals up to maybe 5 satellites all with different coding from different countries, then route it back down to earth and go back again to Africa and your Third World variety before finally we get online. Then after all that, we try to keep our communications – email, video, whatever – under 3 minutes."

"That must take quite a bit of work."

"Hell, yeah, dude. People talk about technology being so fast, but if you really want to set it up to be invisible, it takes serious time and work. That is what I spend most of my time doing. Making and faking bread trails. Anulap helps me out with a lot, of course. My job is not necessarily to be quick, but to be confusing to our opponent and clear and simple to our allies. We use every trick in the book. And, to top it off, like I said, we only send short bursts. Are we completely clean? Probably not, but in the digital world, it is the best we have yet and, so far, we've been invincible."

Rand nodded, taking it all in.

"What about the dark web?"

"Sometimes, we use it, to leave a clue or communicate, but it can make things very complicated. The dark web isn't all it is cracked up to be. Yeah, I've left a couple of messages here and there on boards, but you can't get anywhere near the anonymity we get with using satellites, false emails, hyperlinks, all that. The key is to make the trail long enough, hard enough to follow and then by the time they've gotten to the end – bam, it's gone. Get it?"

"Yeah, I do. But, I've got a question, Declan."

"Sure, bro."

"You said safe houses and headquarters. How many other operations are there exactly on, well, our side?"

"I'm not exactly sure."

"But, aren't you the communications officer?"

"Yeah, it's kind of a bummer. I've only been here like six months so I guess I'm not to be trusted with everything yet. I think I heard something about a location out west. Maybe something else in Canada. I'm not sure, bro. I mean, I get messages to send out and emails to send them to, but I don't get all the details."

There was a distinct nervousness in his voice now, Rand, noticed. Was it cabin fever? Frustration?

"But how does that work? I mean, you must have a general idea of where you are sending these messages, right?"

"Let me break it down for you. Let's say you live in New York and, well, I live here. I won't send you an email to New York. I will send an email to, let's see, somewhere in Oregon. Then that email will have a code in it which will be deciphered and sent – on another email address – to outside Nairobi, then re-coded again and sent to a virtual address, email, site, whatever, in West Virginia, understand?"

CHAPTER NINE

W as it day or night? The lamp was still on by his bed. He was still dressed, the clothes sticking to his body, sweaty, his mouth dry. He remembered talking with Declan. Coming back to his room to rest. Then what? He must have fallen asleep. He sat up, rubbed his shoulder, still sore, but it was even less painful than earlier in the day. He walked to the door.

The hall empty. All silent. He took the stairs to the main floor.

He was greeted by the sight of Hope sitting at the dining table, her legs curled under her, both hands clasping a coffee cup. A man sat across from her. The epitome of a Southern mountain man. Burly. Big. Camouflaged trucker cap pulled tight over shaggy brown hair. Stubble of red beard on his tanned face. Overalls. Stalwart hiking boots. Looked to be in his late 40s.

"Hey Rand, how are you?" Hope asked.

"Fine," he said. "What time is it?"

She glanced at her watch. "9 p.m."

"Wow. I didn't mean to sleep that long. I guess I missed supper."

"No problem, I got you a plate saved," the man said, a distinct Piedmont accent. "We haven't been introduced," he stood, lumbered over and shook Rand's hand. "I'm Shane. My wife and I – well, I guess you could say – help run this cabin," then with an eye towards Hope, "though it usually runs us. But nice to meet you, Rand. Take a seat there with Ms. Hope. I knew when you woke you'd be hungry, so unlike these other knuckleheads who said you could just eat cereal and fruit, I decided to set aside some real dinner for you."

"I appreciate that."

"Of course, of course. Us big men have to eat, right?" He didn't wait for an answer, but pulled a covered plate from the refrigerator and slid it in the microwave. "It was my night to cook, so it isn't anything fancy. Just some black-eyed peas, green beans, cornbread and country fried steak. Will that work for you?"

"Yes sir," Rand said. "I haven't had anything like that to eat, well, in a long time."

"Good man, I knew I would like this guy. He may be from Georgia, but that is a hell of a lot closer than the rest of y'all," a wry smile on the man's face as he extracted the plate from the microwave and handed it to Rand. "Plate's a bit hot, but the food should be warmed just right. If you need anything, holler. I'm going to let you two have some privacy. Tea's in the fridge if you want some."

"Thanks, Shane."

The man gave a thumbs up and disappeared down the hall.

The food was warmed just right and the scent of warm nostalgia wafted through the air. His grandmother had cooked this type of food quite a bit growing up, but since he moved out from under her roof, finding good Southern food wasn't easy. There were lots of chains that claimed to have authentic Southern food, but it was usually straight from the can or the freezer. His own cooking skills were born straight out of bachelorhood 101, a pastiche of Hamburger Helper, frozen dinners and, on occasion, a bagged salad.

"Hungry?" Hope asked, watching amused as Rand dug into the food.

"Yes, sorry about my lack of manners. I am starving and this is good. Real good."

"Don't eat so fast, remember –"

"Yes, I remember, eat slow."

"So, how was your meeting with Declan?"

"Good, I guess. As good as those meetings can go," he said between mouthfuls. "Question, though. So this guy is the communications guru and all, but he says, most of the time he doesn't even know what or to where he is sending information."

A small sigh. "That's right. He's new, you might say. Only been with us for a few months, didn't go through the whole orientation, so, yes, we're just bringing him along slowly. We needed an IT guru, and he was the best we could find on short notice. He is good at what he does though."

Rand nodded. Hope sipped on her coffee and he ate in silence. Finally finished. He stretched his arms behind his head.

"That was delicious. I owe that man a huge thanks."

"Good. I am sure he will welcome it. He says, 'us Yankees' don't appreciate good food. How about some fresh air?"

"Sounds good. I hate being cooped up without any windows."

CHAPTER TEN

The two of them on the porch. Standing. Under a sky glittering with stars. All the stars you can't see in the city, Rand thought. Across the mountains, he could see the occasional yellow light of a window from a cabin or the red winking of a radio tower, but otherwise, all was darkening. Rand tried not to sigh. Waited for a sign from Hope. Anything. He glanced at her. Poised. Still. Hands on the deck rail. Eyes on the mountains.

"So, Hope. What's up? I mean, I don't mean to be so straightforward, but I need to know something. Anything. Like I said earlier, I thought we had a connection. Some chemistry. Now, things are awkward. Distant."

"Nothing has changed, Rand. I just have a lot to juggle right now."

"A lot to juggle? You think I'm not juggling a lot? I mean come on. Was there – is there anything to us – or," the words out before he had a chance to reel them in, "were you just using me as a means to an end?"

She wheeled on him. Arms at her side. Hands clinched.

"You don't get it, do you?"

"Get what? The fact that my life has been taken away from me. The fact that there is no redo. No Control Z. No rewriting this fucked up script. What don't I get Hope? Don't talk to me about getting anything. Good God, I've been awake for less than a day and you're telling me what I get or don't get?"

"It wasn't supposed to happen like this."

"I don't know what 'it' is, but, yeah, trust me, I can assure you it wasn't supposed to happen like this. I was supposed to be going out to the pub or taking my grandmother out for dinner on a night like this, not here in the Hotel California."

"No. You don't get you. You. You were never supposed to be the one who brought down Austria. We don't have people like you working with us. We are academics and scientists and researchers. And then you, you come along. The Wild Card. You're supposed to be the black sheep," and then she closed her eyes and spat out the words. "And, now, everyone around here treats you like the damn White Knight. And I'm sorry, Rand, I'm sorry, but I resent you for that. And I know I shouldn't, but I do."

She was crying. No gush of tears. Just a few solid drops slipping down from shut eyes. Her face aimed toward the ground so he couldn't see.

"Hope, Hope," he said softly, reaching out to hug her.

"Don't touch me, Rand."

"But, Hope, it wasn't me who brought down anything. It was us. You saved me. Have you forgotten?"

She began to wipe away the tears from her cheeks. "But, that's not the way anyone sees it. I had been working for years to do what you did in less than a week."

"But, why are you mad, then? You wanted it done. It got done. That's all that matters, right?"

"You just don't understand, Rand."

Then she turned and left him. Alone. The stars glittering back at him in a stoic silence.

CHAPTER ELEVEN

He had succumbed to the tomb-like sensory deprivation of his room and slept. Then woke, several times in the early morning. Had no idea what time it was. Should he get up? Should he wait? He strained to hear movement in the halls. Nothing. Finally after shifting between wakefulness and dozing, he jettisoned any idea of rest and switched on the lamp.

The same clothes as the day before rumpled on the floor beside him. He slipped them on. The leg still sore, but more agile. He raised his arms in the air. Still a pinch in his shoulder, but already more flexible. Balled his fists. Could feel strength returning in both arms.

Climbed the steps to the main floor. No one at the kitchen table. A clock on the microwave blinked out 5:47 a.m. in green digits. Good. He had not slept in. Glanced around the kitchen. Found an old coffee maker. A lonely banana on the counter. Cereal in the cupboards. Soon, a strong cup of coffee in his hand. Breakfast. Alone. He watched the day begin, the sun leisurely climbing behind the mountains.

A rustle down the hallway. Muffled words. Running water. Sounds of steps. Shane appeared, walking down the hall, already dressed in what looked like the same clothes as the day before.

"Morning, friend," he whispered. "Dadgum, you're an early riser."

"Not usually. Just couldn't sleep. I need a clock in that room."

"No clock? Sorry about that. I'm sure I can find one around

here. If not, I've to run into town again later today."

"I thought y'all usually didn't go out in public too much? The whole Omaha retiree thing and all that."

"Shoot, we usually don't, and that's the way I like it, but Hope has something real important she's working on, I gather. This morning, I found a note outside my door that we needed to head in this afternoon. Who knows? See you made some coffee? Mind if I get a cup?"

"Sure, of course, it's your house," Rand said. "Hope you don't mind. I was just awake and hungry and, I am not a nice person without coffee."

The man laughed, "Me too, buddy, me too."

CHAPTER TWELVE

Rand had finished breakfast and was sharing a second pot of coffee with Shane. Had given the man time to wake up before peppering him with questions.

"Any idea on what I should do now?" He asked, after watching Shane finish his third cup of coffee.

"I can't help you there. I stay up here all the time. I've only been downstairs one time to help deliver some computer equipment...sorry, I don't know what to tell you."

"I reckon I'll go back to my room and read. They gave me a ton of books to read."

"Yeah, I pegged you for a reader."

"Why's that?"

"You know the saying, 'People that like to read are always a little fucked up'?"

"Pat Conroy wrote that, right?"

"You got it, buddy. But, don't worry I like to read too. Maybe I'll see you around lunch."

CHAPTER THIRTEEN

"Even parting your hair on a different side, wearing glasses or not wearing glasses, adopting a stoop, or walking proudly can help in disguises."

The words were from the French espionage book. A simple trick. But, perhaps it could work in a pinch. If these tricks worked over 200 years ago, they must still work now, at least to some extent.

Rand's stomach grumbled. He wondered what time it was. Had left his door open all morning, anticipating to see someone walk by. Anyone to give him direction on what to do.

"Work at adopting regional accents. If you are in Brittany, you want to sound like you are a native. If you are in Lorraine, adopt that accent. If you are in a foreign country, you should already be a master of that language and fluent. If, by chance, you find yourself in a foreign country and have a small chance of blending in with the populous, you might try to adopt the carriage and manner of a confused and eager merchant. One way to accomplish this is –"

A shuffling in the hall. The shape of Dunkel filled his doorway.

"Hey, good morning doc," Rand called out.

"Ah, good morning to you Rand. And how are you today?" The toothy smile. The hands clasped together.

"I'm good. Much better than yesterday. I can't believe how much better my body feels. And, my mind, thank God, is less clouded."

"Ah, yes, the effects of the sedative leaving your system is a very good thing. Drink lots of water. You must be revived. So, no attacking me with a desk lamp today?"

"No, sorry, no desk lamp today. Apologies about that, I –"

"No need to apologize, I just like to make a joke when I can."

"Ha, me too." Rand forced a dry laugh. "Good one. Do you know where Hope is?"

"Ah, she is probably still sleeping. She was up until way past 3 a.m. in the communications center. I was helping her with some ideas on a communique, but then I had to go to bed. I do not have the stamina of you young people. But she should be up soon. All these time zones. They take such havoc upon us. Our senses. Our minds. Of course, the best way to trick the mind is daylight. But, then we do most of our work underground. Ironic, no?" Rand could tell the man did not expect an answer, let him continue. "Okay, then, I am off to lunch. Will you join me?"

"I think I'll wait a bit longer," he said, ignoring his hunger, holding out optimism for a visit from Hope.

CHAPTER FOURTEEN

"Rand, I'm sorry about last night."

The words tumbled out of Hope's mouth. Slowly, almost jaggedly, as if she had been conscripted to say them. Rand sat. Waited for more. They were back on the deck. A late afternoon lunch. Fruit. Egg salad sandwiches. The salty tang of potato chips. Rand sipping on a sweet tea, Hope on a Coca-Cola. She had stopped by his room shortly after Dunkel left. The two had paired off immediately upstairs, grabbing their plates and secluded themselves outside.

"Well?" She asked. "Do I get an acknowledgment or anything? What else do you want me to say?" Her voice sounded almost pleading, any ego now absent.

"I don't know, Hope. I don't know. Sure, of course, I forgive you. We all say things we don't mean to, I am a living example of that. I just didn't expect you to be so angry."

"I know, Rand. There is a lot going on right now. I, I guess I am hesitant to commit to anything with you because I don't know where this," and she gestured around them, "is going. I don't know what's next for our group. And I don't want to become attached just to be taken away."

"And I thought I had walls," Rand said, then trying to recoup, "But, I don't mean that in a bad way. I understand. You know about my parents. I grew up keeping people at arm's length after their death. I mean, I had a few friends on the football team, made some friends in college, but I wasn't exactly mister outgoing.

But, look at us. We're walking on the knife's edge everyday now. I mean, in Austria, here, wherever. Any of us could be snuffed out in a wink. Do I really want to die in wonder? Or in what ifs? No, I've decided that life is too short. I don't know what's next. With us. With anything, but damn, I would rather go out open-hearted, or in love, or with someone, than alone. And, right now, in case you haven't noticed there's not a lot of options around here unless Dunkel is open to forming some type of relationship."

She relented a half-smile.

"Okay, okay. Listen, I've got to run into town with Shane to the post office –"

"Yeah, he told me."

She lifted a hand.

"When I get back, let's go for a hike. Maybe around sunset. There is a river at the foot of this mountain I told you about, remember? We can walk down there and swim or something."

"Or something? I knew there was a romantic in there somewhere. A picnic. Maybe some wine? Swimming. Sounds like I need to be ready to recite a Keats poem."

"Don't get too far ahead of yourself," she said, a seductive glint in her eyes. "While I'm gone why don't you take Declan down some lunch? I'm sure he is hungry and would love to talk to you and show you some more of his gadgets."

CHAPTER FIFTEEN

"**B**ro! Hooking me up!" Declan stood and raised his hands in a mock bow to Rand whose hands cradled a plate full of two egg salad sandwiches, a bag of Doritos and a Coke.

"Sure, enjoy."

"Take a seat. I've got something cool, I pulled up just for you today."

Rand sat in the chair next to Declan and watched the man punch keys on his keyboard with one hand while holding the sandwich with the other. The posture reminded Rand of the reporters who liked to eat at their desk in the newsroom. He could never quite figure out the purpose. Crumbs in keyboards. Greasy phones. The sound of chewing. He imagined some of it was the civility his grandfather had embedded in him. A gentleman should never talk while chewing or eat at his desk. Rand just thought the idea of eating while working was bad for his digestion. If the habit bothered Declan, he didn't show it.

"Bro, great sandwich. Shane always does it right. You want a chip?"

"No thanks," Rand said. "So what have you got for me?"

"Check it out duder."

Declan punched in a few more keys. Jiggled his mouse. An overhead shot maximized on the monitor.

"I was able to hack into a satellite and capture a still shot of this a couple of hours ago. Now, look."

He zoomed in. Rand saw mountains. Slate slabs interspersed among layers of green foliage. A patch of white scattered here and there. Gleaming snow. Declan zoomed in more. Rand saw a river. Or was it a road?

"Check this out, Rand."

Declan switched to 3D mode. The image converted. Declan guided the cursor through a valley.

"Recognize this, bro?"

"No, not really."

"The Central Alps. Austria. Come on dude. Now, here it is."

Declan nudged the mouse. Rand watched as the green foliage turned to brown and then to grey. The trees begin to thin. Then change. Blown back, crushed like matchsticks, scattered. The ground now black. Treeless. A colossal hole in the side of a mountain.

"Got it?" Declan asked.

"No, what is it?"

Declan zoomed out to an overhead view. The image now obvious. A huge crater hole on the side of a mountain. The landscape around it burnt, blistered and torn apart.

"This is it, my man. Your handiwork. This is what you did in Austria."

Rand was quiet. Did not know what to say. The devastation. The magnitude. Almost felt a half-sentimental sadness for the trees. Stared in disbelief at the burnt ground. Thought about the people who were inside The Castle when it exploded.

"Pretty cool, huh, I figured you hadn't quite seen it from this angle, the –"

Declan's words were interrupted by a foghorn like sound that pulsed through the room to the rhythm of a car alarm.

"What's that?" Rand asked, his voice barely audible above the noise.

"The alarm system. That's strange? I ran a diagnostic last week and everything checked out." Declan said. "Let me check."

He sat the sandwich on the edge of the desk. Fingers punching manically at the keyboard. The screen divided into quadrants. CCTV cameras at locations around the cabin. Everything looked status quo. The driveway empty. The deck on the exterior of the house vacant. The forest still, except for the usual breeze in the trees. Not even a raccoon or deer in sight. A serene summer afternoon in Northwest Alabama.

"What happened?" Rand asked.

"I don't know," Declan said. "Maybe an animal tripped it, but I can't see anything. Damn it."

The alarm did not stop. Rand felt his heart rate increase, his hands clenched the side of the chair. Watched Declan scroll back through the screen once again. Rewound the video. Then Rand saw it. A blip. A second where a black flash filled the screen.

"There it is," he said.

"What?"

"Rewind. I saw something."

Declan hesitated, then rewound. Played. Rand saw it again.

"Stop, there it is."

Declan paused on the frame. The camera by the main road.

"Look," Rand said. "There is a pause in the screen right there. A black out. Some kind of skip."

Overhead, they heard a fast flurry of footsteps, the floor creaking under the weight. Then a muffled boom. Rand felt the vibrations shimmer down the walls. Heard the muzzled chatter of machine guns. Damn it. He stood. What to do? What to do? Then he remembered. The bathroom door. The backpacks. The tunnel.

"Let's get out of here," he said to Declan, his body already moving toward the door. As he stepped into the hall, the elevator door opened. A cloud of smoke billowed out. Damn. He was unarmed. Nothing. Not even his cane. He stood transfixed. Heard coughing. A figure emerged from the shaft. It was Dunkel. One hand in front of him waving the smoke away. Another hand clutching a Glock. A bright blotch of red on the shoulder of his white lab coat.

"Dunkel?" Rand asked. "Dunkel, what the hell is going on?"

"They found us," he said, sputtering out the words, between breaths.

"How?"

Dunkel waved him off, the cough wracking his frame.

"I don't know. Who knows? We need to go. To leave. Come, help me with this," he said, turning back toward the elevator.

"What? What can I do?"

"This," Dunkel said. "My right arm is my good arm. It is gone. Broken, I am sure. Shattered. I can't aim. Here. Take my gun. Shoot the control panel in the elevator. We need to disable it as much as possible."

"Just shoot it?"

"Unless you know your way around electronics and shorting the insides out, yes, shoot it."

Rand looked over his shoulder to find Declan. Wanted to ask if he had any experience with electrical engineering. Could not see him. Where was he?

"Do it!" Dunkel said. "Now."

The doors began to close. Rand wedged a foot in. The sensor beeped. They opened again.

"But, wait, Hope? Where's Hope?"

"I do not know, Rand. She went into town. I do not know what happened to her or anyone. Now, we just need to leave. Here." Dunkel thrust the gun into Rand's hand, blood now spilling down his coat, dripping from his forearm.

"What about Hope? Your wound? We need to fix that wound, I –"

"Enough!" Dunkel shouted. A fierce bear of a yell Rand never would have expected from the doctor. "Do you not understand? They are coming to kill us. Forget about Hope. Forget about me, just do it!"

Rand stepped into the elevator. The stench of burnt electrical wiring and spent bullets filling the air in an unholy bouquet. Aimed the gun at the control panel. Fired off one shot. Two shots. Three shots. Four shots. Blue flames spat from the panel. Small sparks dancing. A white noise filled his ears. The echo of the gunshot loud and rendering him half-deaf.

"What else?" He yelled.

"That should do it, mi amicus. I have already sealed off the stairs" he replied. "Nothing to do now, but leave."

CHAPTER SIXTEEN

R and's hand was shaking as he tugged the key from his pocket.

It slid into the lock. He opened the door, lifted an arm to help Dunkel who dismissed him.

"I am fine, but thank you. It is my arm that is gone. My legs are fine."

Closed the door behind them. Where the hell was Declan? Rand hesitated. Heard shouting from somewhere. Rand opened the door and peered out.

"Declan!" He yelled. "Declan!"

"We can't wait," Dunkel said.

Rand turned. Shut the door behind him. Looked at Dunkel. The bleeding had not stopped. His arm cloaked in crimson. His face was ashen. He slumped against the wall.

"You must go, Rand. You must go, now."

"Shit. I don't want to leave you here."

Dunkel gave a sad smile. "It is okay. My journey ends here. My arm is gone. Defunct. They hit a major artery. I can't stop this bleeding. Just do me one favor."

Rand nodded.

"Hand me my backpack."

"What's your color?"

"Brown."

Rand reached over and lifted the bag from the hook.

"Good, now open my bag. Inside you will find three grenades.

Give them to me."

Rand unzipped the bag. Sifted. A jacket, SAT phone, change of clothes, passport. Then there they were at the bottom. Three. He lifted them out gently. Handed them to Dunkel who was now sitting, legs splayed out, back against the wall. His head leaned back. Eyes fluttering. Mouth agape.

"Dunkel?" Rand whispered.

"Thank you," Dunkel said, his voice now raspy, breathing shallow. "Now, I will have a mirandum for them if they find me."

"Mirandum?"

"Ah," a cough. "The old ways come back at the end. The Latin, mi amicus. Mirandum. It means surprise."

The sound of a key sliding into the lock. Rand flinched. Half-lifted the gun. It opened. Declan.

"Where the hell have you been?" Rand said.

"I had to set up, set up the self-destruct system."

"I almost left your ass."

Declan didn't say anything. Looked at Dunkel on the floor. Back to Rand. A strange look on his face.

"First time seeing death?" Rand asked, didn't wait for a response. "Welcome to the fucking club. It sucks. Grab your pack. We're getting out of here."

Declan stood still.

"Let's go," Rand said, lifting his own backpack from the hook, slinging it over his shoulders. Then he heard the voice, barely audible, hushed.

"Rand, Rand."

He turned. Dunkel had angled his head toward him. A thin smile on his face. Rand squatted. Leaned in. Towards the man's mouth.

"Verum in Aeternum."

"Verum in Aeternum," Rand repeated back, his family's motto, 'forever true.'

"Stay it, Rand," another cough.

"Stay it?"

"Forever true. Now flee mi amicus. Run."

CHAPTER SEVENTEEN

They descended through the tunnel. Rand driving. The windows down. Rand feeling the moist coolness around them. A breeding ground for stalagmites and stalactites one day. He remembered hiking in the Raccoon Caverns outside of Chattanooga, Tennessee on a lark of a Saturday in February when he was in high school. Cocky, bold, unafraid. He and his old classmate, Adam Scott, had made the two-hour drive from Atlanta full of bravado. Both squeezed into Rand's green Camry. They had a bottle of wine in the backseat to commemorate their spelunking adventures afterwards. That was before they went in the caves. Pitiless dark. Cramped. Clammy. He had only felt claustrophobic once in his life and it was then. Afterwards, there was no joyous celebration of wine. Rather, a guzzling of the maroon liquid. An anesthetic to cool off his fevered head, to try to push some of the anxiety back from his brain.

He almost felt that way now. The car rushing tightly through the tunnel, the walls close, too close, on each side. But at least it was lit. The strand of old yellow light bulbs dancing overhead, their teeth strung to a rusted wire. Finally, the tunnel began to level off. Rand pumped the brakes hard, slowed down to a crawl. Then, there it was. An old garage door stared back at them in the glow of their headlights.

"Get out," Rand said to Declan. "Open the door."

Declan sat still, staring ahead.

"Come on, get out," Rand's irritation rising higher now at the lack of speed and constant hesitation.

"Okay, okay, bro."

Rand watched as he slowly walked to the door. Pushed and pulled on the handle. Rand was about to get out of the car and do it himself, when Declan finally was able to lift it up, faint daylight from the forest creeping in. Rand gunned the car out of the tunnel and onto what Hope had generously called a dirt road, though it resembled more of an abandoned wagon trail.

"Come on, close the doors behind you. Get in."

Again, Declan slowly pushing the doors back into place. A sheath of moss and ivy fell over them, a camouflage that looked like it had been there for decades.

Declan slid in the car. His face still pale. Rand noticed his hands were shaking.

"Buckle up," Rand said. "If this is like any other dirt road in the mountains it is going to be a bumpy ride."

CHAPTER EIGHTEEN

The river swept by to their left, a bank leading up to the side of the mountain on their right. Washboard ripples and minor potholes underneath kept the car bouncing joylessly, the grate of the undercarriage and strain of the engine an inglorious soundtrack to their drive.

"It shouldn't be much further," Rand said. "She said it was about half a mile."

Declan was silent. Rand glanced over to see his hands holding onto the dashboard. Knuckles white. Mouth agape.

The road began to level out. They must be getting near the summit. A parting of light ahead. The tunnel of canopy receding. And then there they were.

"All right," Rand said. "Let's get ready."

He reached into the backseat, grabbed his backpack and opened it. Pulled out the Glock, made sure it was loaded. Laid it in his lap. Extracted the SAT phone.

"All right, Declan, open the glove box."

Declan leaned forward, almost as if in a daze, opened the glove box, pulled out a black plastic box. No key. No combination. Just a latch. Rand took it from him. Whatever was going on in Declan's mind, he didn't have time to psychoanalyze. They needed to move, and move now.

The box clicked open. Inside was a black device. Rand thought he recognized it.

"So, this looks like a basic radar detector. Okay, that works,"

Rand said before attaching it to the dashboard.

"Are, are you going to keep your gun out, like in your lap?"

"Hell, yes. These people…if it is them, and I don't know who else it would be, they don't play games, Declan. And I don't take chances...at least not anymore. Oh, and speaking of chances, Hope," he paused momentarily. What had happened to Hope? Was she in town? Was she back at the house? Where was she?

"Dude? You okay?"

Rand blinked. Felt a tear welling up. Shoved it back. Straightened his back. Save the sentimentality. Focus. "Yeah, I'm fine. Hope, she said there were directions on what to do in the glove box. Do you see anything else in there?"

"Yeah dude. Here."

Declan handed over an envelope. Rand opened it. Inside was a map of Alabama and one slip of paper. Hand-written. Of course, Rand thought.

Turn on phone.

Dial 1-33-23-9971

At tone, punch in 33.

You will hear a beep.

Instructions to follow.

Rand lifted the SAT phone out of his backpack. Punched in the numbers. Were they a European area code? African telephone number? There was a long pause. Static shot in and out the earpiece. Then a tone. Rand punched in the number 33.

A metallic voice answered:

"What's your color?"

"Color?" Then Rand remembered. The backpack. His color. "Yes, yes, this is Green."

"Good. Are you alone?"

"No."

"What other color is with you?"

Rand cupped the receiver, looked at Declan, mouthed, 'What's your color?'

"What?" Declan asked.

"What's your color damn it? Your backpack color."

"Oh, uh, yellow."

Rand lifted his hand off the receiver.

"Yellow. Yellow is the other color."

"Copy that. Green use Passport for Waverly Hall. Yellow use passport for Marcus Benedict. Proceed to Huntsville International Airport. Charter jet under the name of Cunningham will be waiting. Do you copy?"

"Yes."

"Good. Over and out."

"But, but," Rand said, but the line was dead.

"Shit," he muttered, looked at Declan. "Well, get your passport ready. You're going to be Marcus Benedict and I am Waverly Hall, actually a nice name. Sounds very Anglo and proper. Non-threatening. Hell, I might keep it."

"What are we going to do?"

"To Huntsville we will go. Can you read a map?" Rand said, stuffing the phone inside the backpack he dropped in the backseat.

Declan hesitated. "Yeah, bro. I guess. I mainly use, you know, like GPS, my phone and stuff."

"Well, this is pretty simple. If you need help, let me know. Otherwise you navigate and I'll drive. Got it?"

"Got it."

An 18-wheeler rumbled past, its diesel exhaust belching thick plumes into the sky. Rand checked the rear view mirror. Nothing behind them but trees and the rough splinter of the road. He looked both ways on the highway.

"Well, here goes nothing."

He pressed the pedal down to the floorboard. Gravel spat up behind them and they peeled out onto the road.

CHAPTER NINETEEN

Huntsville was the antithesis of a mid-sized city in the South. In the post-World War II era, it became a mecca for space engineering. Wernher von Braun had been the most prominent scientist in the emerging U.S. space program, but he was only one of 118 former German engineers and rocket gurus who made the area their home. During the next few decades, that group worked with their U.S. counterparts to engage in a myriad of space and rocket projects, including, putting astronauts on the moon.

The city had reaped the rewards, not only of visibility, but also economically boasting one of the highest per capita incomes in the state and evolved into a high-tech hub. Finding a charter flight in less than an hour to fly non-stop might not have been par for the course, but was much easier than other towns its size in The South. All that came in handy for Rand and Declan as they veered onto the main road leading to the airport. They had taken a circuitous route without incident. By the time they reached the outskirts of Huntsville, the sun was starting to dip in the west.

Rand had tucked the gun back into the backpack and it rested on the backseat of the car.

Rand followed the signs to the charter flights and stopped the car at the security gate.

A man in a smart, starched white uniform, cradling an iPad, walked out from a guardhouse to meet them.

"Good evening, gentlemen."

"Evening sir," Rand replied. "We're here for a charter flight. Our pilot, er, Captain Cunningham might have radioed ahead and given us clearance."

"Let's see. Sounds familiar," the man held his iPad up, ran his finger over it. "Yep, there it is. Captain Cunningham. Two passengers. You gentleman have your I.D.s with you?"

"Yes sir," Rand said, stretching his arm out of the window clutching both passports.

The man stared at the passports.

"So you must be Waverly?"

"That would be me, sir," Rand said.

"Small world. That is a rare name, but I've got a cousin named Waverly. Family name?"

"Ah, yes sir. It was my grandfather's," easy lies spilling from his tongue.

"Well, good name. I have no idea how my cousin got his name, but it is unique. Well, enough of that. This looks good to go. Captain Cunningham procured an express pass for you gentlemen so you can drive straight onto the tarmac. He's busy running final inspection points."

"Great. Thank you, sir."

CHAPTER TWENTY

Rand had thought flying first-class as the ultimate luxury, but that idea dissipated when he boarded, "Cirrus Seeker" a shiny white Lear-jet 35. Six leather chairs in the cabin with ample legroom. A mini-fridge complete with cold cuts, snacks, wine and soft drinks. A tiny bar and a variety of small tables lined the walls. The captain, a jovial man in his 50s with ginger hair and a matching mustache had welcomed them and offered to hoist their luggage on board, until he discovered they had none with the exception of their backpacks. If he suspected anything amiss, he didn't show it. Instead, he made sure they knew their way around the cabin and apologized for not having a stewardess on such short notice.

"Gentlemen, if you don't have any questions, we're going to take off. I generally leave the door to the cockpit closed so my guests can have privacy. If you need anything, just knock," he said.

"Sounds good," Rand said.

The cockpit door closed. Rand sank into the seat. Spread his legs out and buckled his seat belt. Stole a glance at Declan who still looked nervous. Or was it indecisiveness? Rand couldn't decipher the expression on his face.

"Where are we heading, Rand?"

"The people I called filed the flight plan, I imagine. I didn't ask as I thought it would make us, well, look like we shouldn't be here. Make sense?"

"Yeah, I guess so."

"We should be fine as long as we act like we know what we're doing. Most of these charter flight pilots are like limo drivers. They get paid to be discreet. They don't typically ask questions or care about their cargo or what their cargo is up to. Trust me, we're probably the tamest he's had in here."

"Good evening gentlemen, I'll go ahead and make this official," the voice emanated from speakers embedded in the ceiling overhead, "Welcome aboard, Flight 815. Huntsville, Alabama to Martinsburg, West Virginia. We are ready for take-off and the runway is clear. I've got us on a bearing north by northeast. We should be climbing to a cruising altitude of about 30,000 feet. Our time in the air should be about 3 hours, but we do have some nasty storms in Tennessee and western North Carolina we will be watching. If you need anything, press the button next to your seat or just knock on the door. Thanks for flying with Captain Max Cunningham."

CHAPTER TWENTY-ONE

A s much as he adored their golden towers and velvety silver fields, Rand had grown weary of gazing at the clouds. His eyes itched, his mind was beginning to turn off, his head bobbing toward his chest. So he had followed Declan's lead, rested his head back against the seat and closed his eyes. Just three hours to their destination. He needed sleep and it came slow, but, at last did come weaving a shawl over him, shielding the world and his worries behind a thin drape.

A jarring bump woke him and he felt himself rise in his seat, the seatbelt tightly gripping his waist, pulling him back down.

"Sorry about that gentlemen," the voice came in overhead. "Just a pocket of turbulence we're going through right now, some of that nasty weather I thought we might run into. I'm going to climb above it and we should be back to smooth flying in about ten minutes or so. In the meantime, go ahead and buckle those safety belts and hold onto your drinks."

The plane tilted back and Rand heard the engines purr louder as they began to ascend. Outside the windows, wisps of white and gray clouds swept by. Rand felt like they were in a tunnel of wraiths, trying to escape their reaching hands. He turned his head back to the cabin, the sight outside the window too ethereal, too un-nerving. It was only then that he noticed Declan's seat empty. Saw a pair of legs on the floor beside him. Rand tried to crane his neck back as the plane rose. Called out.

"Declan? Declan? You okay?"

A mumble. Rand could not decipher the words over the increasing noise of the engines.

"You okay?"

No reply. Then the voice from the speaker.

"Okay, just another minute and we'll be above this. Hang on boys."

The plane banked to the port-side as it continue to rise. A flood of sunshine lit up the cabin. The plane leveled off. Rand glanced out the portal. A field of clouds below them, molted grey interspersed with billowy whites, small bursts of lightening dancing through them, but all around them and above, nothing but a rich blue.

Rand unbuckled his seat belt. Stood. Steadied himself. Stared at the body.

Declan was face down in the aisle. Both arms laid out in front of him. A syringe in one hand, its needle gleaming in the golden sunlight. Rand knelt beside him, slipped the syringe out of the hand. Cradled it in his palm. Rolled Declan over. The eyelids flickered open. Once. Twice. Then wide. Rand saw fear. Panic?

"Declan, are you okay. What happened?"

The eyes blinked again. Looked around.

"I..I...I don't know. Did we fly into a storm or something?"

"Yeah, we did. Hit a pocket of turbulence, but we're fine now. Good pilot, I guess. Thank goodness I was strapped in. What were you doing?"

Rand saw him look toward his hand. Noticed the surprise when he didn't see the syringe. His head turned back to meet Rand's gaze.

"Uh, nothing, bro. Just getting up to get something to drink, you know?"

"Bullshit. Why the syringe?"

"Syringe? What syringe?" Then a rise in the voice, "Are you going crazy? I got up to get a Coke, then I don't remember. I was knocked out, I guess. You should be helping me. Get me some aspirin or ice, instead of talking about a syringe."

Rand opened his hand, lifted the syringe in front of Declan's face.

"This syringe. What's going on? Are you using? What is this? Talk."

"Rand, I'm sorry man."

"Sorry?"

Declan punched Rand in the temple which knocked him off balance and onto his back. Rand surprised at the strength. Shocked at the punch. Then Declan was up. Half-standing, half-swaying in the aisle. A predatory look in his eye Rand had not seen before. Fists raised, staring down at Rand.

"What the hell is going on?" Rand asked.

"Hand it over."

"Hand over what?"

"Hand over the syringe. Wherever you put it. Hand over the goddamn syringe and let's make this easy."

"Fuck that," Rand said. The syringe still in his right hand. Used his left hand to grab hold of one of the seat's arms and began raising himself up.

Declan looked at him. Watched him stand. A wash of confusion on his face.

"Come on Rand. Hand it over. Let's make this easy."

"Make what easy? What's your game, Declan?"

Declan didn't answer. Instead, a quick uppercut snapped Rand's head back. Rand felt himself falling backwards. He swung out with his right hand, flailing wildly. Then he stopped falling. Hung in the air for a second. The needle had found flesh. The syringe embedded in Declan's arm, Rand hanging on with it, like a climbing axe lodged in the side of a mountain. Declan howled, then fell back with him. Their bodies fell to the floor side by side. A crackling spat through the speaker. Captain Cunningham's voice.

"Is everything okay back there? Is everything okay?"

Rand rolled off of Declan. Dots in front of his eyes. His head swimming. Saw the syringe sticking out of Declan's arm. Half empty. He pulled it out. Declan lay supine. Unconscious, Rand thought, but why take chances. He put a knee on his chest. Declan silent. No motion. No protest. The crackling overhead again.

"I repeat, is everything okay back there?"

Rand stood, left his foot on Declan's back, leaned over and pressed the button for the intercom.

"Yes sir, everything is fine. Just a little tipsy, I think. We had a slight tumble…from the tumbler."

"You boys flying with Jim Beam back there?"

Rand breathed a sigh of relief.

"Well, Jim was here earlier, but now his cousin Johnny Walker is on board with us. Sorry about the bouncing around. We're settling down. My friend just hates flying and needed something to take the edge off."

"All right, all right. But no more of that. Y'all scared the hell out of me for a moment. Just relax, okay. There are some movies back there if you need to take your mind off of something."

"Yes sir. Thanks."

CHAPTER TWENTY-TWO

"Wake up. Wake up."
No response. Then louder.
"I said wake up damn it!"

Rand tossed a few ice cubes from the mini-fridge down the front of Declan's shirt and slapped him on the cheek. Hard. The eyes slowly cracked open.

"Wake up!"

The eyes half opened. Declan looked around. Saw his hands strapped to the seat in a ponderous knot Rand had weaved from a blanket. Rand crouched in front of him, gripping his Ka-Bar. Declan dropped his head. Rand slapped him again.

"Come on Declan or whatever the hell your name is. I need answers. I need them now."

Declan opened his eyes, offered a half sneer.

"You want answers? That's rich. You're in so over your head." Closed his eyes again.

"Okay, feeling groggy? Don't want to answer? We recommend using Rand's wake up call. Guaranteed to work every time."

Rand lifted the blade and held the knife to Declan's ear.

"I am tired of this shit. I have lost patience and you are about to lose an ear. Do you understand? I am done."

Rand pressed the blade against the supple flesh behind the ear lobe. Not enough to cut, but enough for Declan to feel the pin prick sharpness of the blade. He jerked. Eyes open. Rand saw what he wanted now. Fear.

"Now, are you awake?"

Declan nodded.

"Good, cause let's get something straight, bro," he leaned on the word. "I might kill you. I hope not. But, I will make you suffer until you give me what I want. I am not going to just cut off your ear. I will make you feel pain first. Lots of it. And then some."

Rand could barely believe the words coming out of his mouth. And so easily. Maybe it was fear. Maybe the fact that he had never liked this guy. Maybe the fact that he didn't know where Hope was. Maybe tired of being the victim. Or maybe all of it combined.

He saw panic in Declan's eyes. Felt himself losing control. Wanted to stop. But didn't want to stop.

"Yeah, that's right bro. I will make you suffer. Didn't think I had it in me, did you? Guess what? I've had it. What did you hear about me? A good man in the wrong place? A chivalrous man like his grandfather? The whore with the heart of gold shit. Some shit like that. All bullshit and conjecture. You don't know me, Declan. And you set me up. You set Hope up where ever she is," a fleeting sense of sadness, replaced by newborn fury. "My patience is not worn. My patience is worn out. Now tell me what the fuck is going on."

"It's not as easy as you think. The thing is –"

Before he could finish, Rand backhanded Declan with his left hand. Blood spurted from the lips. Rand moved the knife to the man's crotch.

"I'm not playing anymore."

Declan cried out, but Rand punched him in the mouth with the handle of the blade. Stuffed a piece of the blanket he had cut into Declan's mouth. Shoved it in hard.

"Keep your mouth shut, damn it. Shut up. Sorry about the cut lip, here this will help the infection." Rand leaned over and grabbed the bottle of vodka and poured it into the wound. Saw Declan's eyes watering, his body trembling.

Rand didn't want to go any further. Already loathing himself for threatening the man. He wasn't a torturer or a sadist. Hated what he was doing. But he had been sold out by this kid. And Hope too. Where was Hope? What had happened? He shook his head. Had to forget. Just focus. On the now. On the here. Think. He watched Declan's eyes blink rapidly, eyes welling, alcohol and the cut doing their job, the long burn. The drawn out pain.

"Are you ready to talk now?" Rand lifted the bottle above the cut again. "Or shall I sterilize some more?"

Declan nodded.

"Do not yell," Rand ordered. Did not expect a reply.

Rand extracted the cloth from his mouth.

"I – I am sorry Rand."

"Fuck off with the apologies. What is going on? What have you done?"

"I did...what I had to do." Real tears now welling up in the eyes..."I was blackmailed. They threatened my family. My mother...she is in a real mess...needed money, God...just did it, I -"

"You what? Answer the damn question!" Rand's voice rising again.

"Okay, okay. They told me to let them know about the Mentone outpost, you know, the cabin. They wanted to see if you were there. It was a chance meeting. One of those rare Tuesdays I actually got to go into town by myself. I picked up a six pack at the gas station. A man came up to me in the beer aisle. Told me he could fix things with mom. She's real sick, Rand. She doesn't have the money she needs. It's a mess. But this man. He said, he just needed me to give him the details on where we were and how to get in past our security measures and your status. I don't know. We talked for like five minutes. I can't remember everything I told him. But they thought you were there and they wanted you. And Hope, too."

"Why? Why the hell would they want me? Revenge?"

"I don't know Rand. I don't think revenge. They wanted you alive. If that was just revenge, well, they could have made it easier. They could have just asked me to kill you or bombed the place. They wanted you for something else. I don't know what. I'm good with computers, bro, this is all above my head. I was just supposed to be lax about security and then, when they came, they wanted me to subdue you. The syringe. He gave it to me."

More tears.

"This doesn't make sense. Why did you run with me? Why didn't you shoot me up me at the cabin or in the tunnel? Why now?"

"Rand," a cough, "Rand, I panicked. I wasn't armed. I just had this syringe. You went running out of the room, then into the tunnel. I hesitated. Then Dunkel came running down, bleeding everywhere. That freaked me out. Dude, I didn't know what to do. And you wouldn't slow down. You just took off so, all, all I could do was follow along. Everything happened so fast until a few minutes ago…You were just asleep. I waited until now….I'm sorry."

Rand stared into the man's eyes, looking for anything. Was he telling the truth?

"Okay, okay. You waited until now. What were you going to do next?"

"When we landed, I was going to call them, have them come pick you up or whatever."

"So, they don't know where we are?"

"No. They didn't give me a tracking device or anything. Just that syringe. Told me to stay close to you. Then when they raided, to shoot you up. It would make you drowsy or whatever. They would get you then, easy."

"So, you've just followed along since we left. Just waiting. Like a damn jackal."

The veil lifted. Rand could see it. Waiting for Declan in the tunnel. Wondering where he went. Wondering why he was so hesitant to take any action. The constant fear and panic in his eyes. Declan began crying again.

"Stop your crying. You're pathetic," Rand said.

"So, what are you going to do, Rand?" Sniffles.

"You mean what am I going to do with you?" Rand knew what he would do. Despite his misgivings, despite his anger, he could not kill this man. Unarmed. Blackmailed by fear of a dying mother. But, he couldn't let Declan know that. Had to keep up a front. "I don't know what I'm going to do with you. But, first, I need some information. Once again, do they know where we are?"

"No, I swear, bro. I swear."

"How can I trust you?"

"I, I don't know."

"You said you were to contact them when you had me subdued. Did they give you a phone number in case anything happened?"

"Yes. Yes, they did."

"Have you called it?"

"No, when could I? I've been with you the whole time since we left."

Rand thought about it. He was right.

"Okay, then. What is the number?"

"67-90-89-890."

"Say it again."

"67-90-89-890."

"You sure?"

"Yeah, they made me memorize it."

He wasn't lying. Not now. That much Rand knew.

CHAPTER
TWENTY-THREE

Rand stood. Had to gather his thoughts. Stared out the window. A meadow of clouds underneath. Buttery sunlight. Declan still sniffling. Had to make a decision. Pressed the intercom button.

"Captain, this is Waverly, here. We had something come up, can we file a new flight plan?"

"Uh, changing flight plans is not something we usually do, especially in mid-flight. What were you thinking of exactly?"

"Well, my friend is sick. He had an asthma attack. His inhaler is empty. That and the alcohol. He just wants to rest. Call a prescription in. Can we land at the nearest airport and drop him off?"

"Roger that. This is a little unorthodox. Give me a few minutes to check in, but it looks like we might be able to land in Asheville."

"Thanks."

CHAPTER
TWENTY-FOUR

Rand had guided a staggering Declan from the plane to a bathroom stall inside a hangar where he injected him with whatever the hell was in the syringe, then stripped him and poured a bottle of Jim Beam over his clothes.

The image of a misplaced, confused drunk with his head leaning against a dirty cinder block wall was exactly what he wanted to achieve when Declan was discovered. He did his best to wipe his fingerprints from the syringe, the door handle and anything else he thought he touched. He took the money and I.D.s from Declan's pocket, then thinking, what if they had tracking devices on them too? He flushed the money down the toilet. Tossed the I.D.s in the trash can. Took Declan's cell phone. Smashed it with his heel.

The backpack? What to do with the backpack and the clothes? He still didn't know what was in Declan's backpack. Was it booby-trapped? Rigged to explode if it was opened? Programmed to send out a signal? Already tracking? Damned if he was going to find out. He found a trash bin in the hangar. Stuffed it inside. Murmured a prayer that no one would get hurt. He knew it was live or die time, but the ghost of Billy Gallagher, the unfortunate construction worker he had traded an iPhone for an electric razor in Ireland, still haunted him.

He waited at the edge of the vacant hangar, eclipsed in the shadows of the overhang. He reached into his backpack and pulled out the phone.

Dialed 1-33-23-9971

Punched in 33. The beep.

Static.

The metallic voice again.

"Yes."

"Yes, uh, we had a situation develop and I need to reroute our earlier flight plan. I think, the, uh, original destination is compromised."

A silence.

"Understand. New flight plan being filed. New destination configured. Proceed to plane. Contact us again after you've landed."

CHAPTER
TWENTY-FIVE

He walked across the tarmac. Sensed nothing out of the ordinary. Waited for a blue light. An announcement. The skid of car tires. Nothing.

Climbed into the plane. Pulled the hatch up behind him.

"You ready sport?" The captain called back.

"Yep. You got it. Are we okay on the flight plan to the new destination?"

"Yes sir. Just got off the phone and filed it. That was a strange change, but the okay came through in a jiff. And as much as you people pay to keep me on retainer, I don't mind either way."

"You mind if I ride in the cockpit with you the rest of the way?"

"Sure. Always appreciate the company."

"Thanks."

CHAPTER
TWENTY-SIX

Why. Why of all places here?

Presque Isle, Maine.

Rand had never even heard of it. And Isle? He would've thought it was a place off the coast. Maybe a ferry jaunt from Bar Harbor or a long boat ride to an abandoned lighthouse hundreds of miles off the mainland alone and stalwart in the choppy, grey Atlantic.

However, as the plane had circled one of the two runways at Northern Maine Regional Airport, Rand was surprised as he gazed out the cockpit and was met with miles upon miles of woods out one window and rows of fertile farmland and lonely farmhouses out of the other. As they began their descent through the thin, early morning light, Rand saw a moose and her calf galloping away from the runway.

"Captain, where exactly are we?" Then realizing how ignorant that sounded, "I mean, I know where we are, but what can you tell me about this area? This is my first time up here."

"I've only flown in here once before about ten years ago. I actually spent the night somewhere in the city. Had to get some winks. Anyway, not a whole lot to it. Small town. Maybe, I don't know, 10,000 or so people. We're about a half an hour from the Canadian border and about three hours inland. From what I remember, this all used to be farmland up here. Potatoes mainly. For a long time, they had a pretty big Air Force base. It closed down and took about a third of the town with it. I wish I could tell you more, but it was dark when I landed and dark when I woke up. Fine people though. From what I remember, they were real friendly."

"Thanks," Rand said. "I won't be here long, but curious. Always good to know any inside information."

"Yeah, I understand. No sweat. Everybody who flies with me wants an inside scoop. Most of them big businessmen. They just want to know the best restaurants and the best strip clubs, and not exactly in that order," He shook his head. "So you asking about the city? Hell, that's an easy question. Plus, I don't think they have any strip clubs in Presque Isle."

The airplane cruised to a stop.

"Thanks, I appreciate it. And thanks again for making that unscheduled pit stop in Asheville. You know how people can be."

"Trust me. God knows I do. Like I said, you're easy. No drugs, no requests for hookers, just a sick friend. I'm happy."

"So what's next for you?"

"Hell, I don't know. These charter jobs change at the drop of a hat. I'll probably just wait. Should be getting a request in an hour or so."

"Well, I appreciate it," Rand said, fishing a couple of hundred dollar bills out of his pocket and handing them over.

"Hey, I appreciate it. Thanks for the tip. And be careful...whatever you're up to."

God knows what I'm up to, Rand thought. Didn't say anything. Slight nod of the head.

"Take care."

He grabbed his backpack, double checked his pockets for his wallet and sauntered across the faded and cracked airstrip to the arrival gate. The terminal hall was nearly empty. Rand slipped into a bathroom that hadn't been updated since the 1980s, cool teal paint on the walls and off-white tile floors.

Rand ducked inside a stall, pressed the green button on his phone. Pressed 33.

Again, silence. The code. A crackle. Then a series of beeps. Chirps. The same voice as before:

"Meet at Governor's. 1 p.m. every day until contact arrives. Code word is 'Eagle.' Code word is 'Eagle.'"

"Meet at Governor's?" He asked.

No reply. The phone went dead. Nothing.

"Damn," Rand sighed. "Here we go again."

CHAPTER
TWENTY-SEVEN

A man in a grey business suit passed him, busy yammering on his cell phone. A family of four clad in typical American sportswear walked by, their laughter sprinkling in with what Rand guessed was French. In a waiting room was an ensemble of coin-operated TVs. Faded chairs and couches. How bizarre, Rand thought. The last airport he remembered was Shannon Airport in Ireland and, before that, Atlanta's Hartsfield-Jackson, which proudly boasted it was, 'the world's busiest.' Now this emptiness, this sense of deflation, of pop-culture relics.

Finally, he found a woman staffing a counter near the ticket gate.

"Good morning, ma'am," he said.

He was met with a friendly smile and a flip of raven black hair from an alabaster face.

"Good morning," the accent thick, but not unpleasant. It reminded Rand of a mix of Canadian and a girl he once dated from Minnesota. "Can I help you?"

"Yes ma'am. Could you direct me to the taxis?"

"Ma'am," she giggled. "I love it. So cute, you must be from the South. Let me guess, Texas? No, maybe Mississippi?"

Rand smiled.

"No, actually, Georgia," then remembering misinformation, misdirection. "Yeah, uh, Georgia. Georgia, Louisiana."

"Georgia or Louisiana?" She asked.

"No, Georgia, Louisiana, a small town outside of Baton Rouge. Strange name, but a nice place."

"Well, I betcha it is a nice place."

"Yes ma'am."

"There you go again," she said, another flip of the hair. "Okay, anyway, a taxi? We don't have a taxi service at the airport. But, my cousin Joshua drives for City Taxi. I can ring him up for ya. How far you going?"

"Just into Presque Isle."

"You got it," she said.

CHAPTER TWENTY-EIGHT

An old Subaru Outback slowed in front of the gate, coughing ashen exhaust, a magnet stating, 'City Taxi' slapped on the passenger's door. The window rolled down.

"You must be my passenger, eh?" Again, the northern Maine accent, delivered a matter-of-fact, but not unfriendly.

"Yes, sir."

"Great, get in. You need a hand with that bag?"

"No sir, just a backpack. You mind if I ride in the front, I tend to get carsick in the backseat."

"Of course. Whatever you need, you let me know."

Rand lowered himself into the car. Shut the door. The cab driver had a shock of black hair on his head, deep brown eyes and pale skin. He nodded at Rand, but did not offer a hand.

"How you doing? Where you going?"

"Do you know of anywhere called Governor's?"

"Governor's? You mean the restaurant?"

"Uh, sure."

"Oh, you betcha. Governor's. Great food. Best pies in Presque Isle. Probably best pies in the whole county. Big breakfast, too. Man's breakfast, you know, made for working. Good seafood too. You like seafood? You must be hungry to want to go eat there."

"Yes sir, just flew in from," Rand hesitated, "uh, Chicago. Coming up here to meet some friends to hike in Canada… want a hearty meal first."

"Hiking in Canada? Sounds fun. Lots of wildlife around here – moose, ducks, eagles. But watch out for the bears. They aren't vegetarians."

CHAPTER
TWENTY-NINE

Rand tucked into a Philly Steak omelet, a ridiculous cholesterol-laden concoction where the eggs could only be classified as secondary to the meats and cheeses. Toast, home fries and coffee with cream on the side. Though Rand was famished, he tried not to be too absorbed on his breakfast and kept an eye on his surroundings. He had requested the farthest booth from the door, sitting with his back to the wall. And he intensely watched every person who came in. Looking for anything. A look of recognition? Someone out of place? Studious eyes? Nothing. The casual saunter of local businessmen or working farmers and laborers, most who greeted each other by name. No black fatigues. No sleek suits. Nothing.

He had scooped the last of the omelet onto the toast and was sipping on a fresh cup of coffee when he heard a voice behind him.

"How about them Eagle making that trade for a new Quarterback? What they need is a new receiver, not another washed up QB. But that's the Eagle, huh?" An out-of-place accent. Texas? Oklahoma? Not Maine.

Rand felt himself stiffen. Surprised.

Felt a body move past him, sit in the booth in front of him. A worn plaid shirt tucked into a pair of faded jeans. A black cowboy hat perched on the head. A pair of dark brown, almost black, eyes greeted him, embedded into a creased face, etched by sun and wind and something else. Tiny dots of black and white whiskers covered the chin. Rand estimated the man to be in his late 60s.

"I said," the man began again. "How about the Eagle? Terrible roster management, isn't it?"

Rand waited. Remembered. The man could just be a tad off his rocker. It was the Philadelphia Eagles football team. Not the Eagle. But Eagle was the word. He took a chance.

"Yeah, the Eagle are crazy, aren't they?"

"You bet they are," the man surveyed Rand's face, then his plate. "You done eatin'? Good God, you've got an appetite."

"Yes, sir."

"Good, good, follow me out the back."

Rand left a $20 on the table and followed the man through the kitchen. The man amiably waved at the cooks and called out a few greetings before the two slipped out the door and clamored into an old 1980s blue Bronco.

The inside was as rough as the man who drove it. Faded pleather blue seats with rips from overuse. Coffee cups rattling in the floorboard. A thick coat of dust on the dashboard and the smell of stale cigarette smoke.

Rand cracked his window as the engine roared to life.

"At first, I thought my transponder was broken," the man said.

"Pardon me?"

"Transponder. You know. How you guys reach me. That thing hadn't gone off in about five years. I thought I was off all missions. Retired as you might say. Then a few hours ago, about halfway into a dream about Raquel Welch, the damn thing went off. About gave me a heart attack. But I checked it. It was right. You are here."

"Yes sir, my name is –"

"Don't need your name. Don't want your name or the name on your passport or whatever you cooked up unless I need to, okay? I got your code name, that's all that matters right now," he said. He noticed a look of confusion on Rand's face. "You must be new. We all go by colors and code names, mainly birds, sometimes whatever the heck else someone thinks up. But I'm the Eagle. And I know you or as much as I care to. You're the Green Phoenix.

But I'm The Eagle.....The old Eagle, now" he said, gazing ahead on the road, a look of mist and sentimentality in his eyes.

Rand didn't know he was 'The Green Phoenix.' Had not known much at all. His training – if he could even call it that - in Mentone was so fast. So rushed. So short.

"Where are we going?" Rand asked.

The truck was winding through the town, past a tidy Post Office and a string of abandoned diners, traffic sparse in the sleepy post-lunch hour.

"Oh, I've got an old farmhouse, about ten miles north. Beautiful country. It's an old house, but secure as hell. More or less off the grid. I mainly spend my days with my horses and cows, grow some potatoes like everyone else around here…but that's about it. Sell to the locals.....Haven't been on adventure in a long time."

"How long have you lived up here?"

"Oh," the man ran a thumb under his chin. "About 15 years ago, I guess. Had one too many close calls. Had to close out my account, you might say, but you never really leave, you know? So, I stayed on…after the split…kind of a safety net," a clearing of the throat. "But this is good. This has been good. I'm originally from West Texas, so this area speaks to me in a way, kind of like that area, but with potatoes and hell of a lot cooler weather. But it's got that big sky. I love the big sky."

Soon, the shops began to grow more infrequent and they quickly left the city limits. The Bronco turned off the main road and took an unmarked road heading north. Rand glanced out the window, saw long rows of potato plants, stout green vines in a sea of brown. Endless. And then, a change. Mustard fields. A thousand blips of yellow among the thin green stalks. And framing it all was that big sky.

"You live alone?" Rand asked.

"My, my you're a curious cat, aren't you?" The man shot him a mirthful look, "But, yeah. I live alone. Never planned to, but my wife Lucy died about seven years ago. I've been wanting to hang it up myself, you know," he gave Rand a sidewards glance. "You know. Hang up this life. Toss in the chips. Punch my time card for the last time. But, I keep goin'. Like I said, this is good here. Good community, good people, good church-goin' folks. So,

I've been sticking around, takin' it easy. Trying to find my peace in the cows and the lilies in the fields and all that damn poetry. Hang on, it's gettin' ready to get bumpy."

The Bronco veered a sharp right onto a dirt road. Though the man drove slowly, the massive potholes had Rand bouncing up and down like a buoy in an angry sea. The man gunned the engine and swerved back and forth. The truck surged over the last of the holes and sped up a small rise to where a white-washed one-story farmhouse waited. Modest. Well-kept, but lonesome, Rand mused. No great sweeping lawn. No grandiose trees out front or lawn ornaments. Just the house, a few shrubs dotting the grass and behind it, a long wooden fence where Rand could see a few cows grazing. In another world, Rand mused the scene could be a painting by Andrew Wyeth. The Bronco rocked to a stop and jettisoned any artistic notions out of his head.

"Welcome to my place. Not much, but I don't expect you'll be here long. You hungry? Oh hell, of course not. You just ate half of the food at Governor's."

Rand smiled, "Yes sir. Yes, I did." A slight pat to the belly.

"Come on in."

Rand followed The Eagle up a few worn wooden steps. The man pushed the door open.

"You don't even lock your door?"

The man turned around, the door halfway open. "Ain't you figured most stereotypes are true? This is country living. I only keep it locked at night or during the winter to keep the bears out. Plus, who wants to steal anything from this place?"

The flick of a light switch. A modest parlor complete with a grandfather clock standing in a corner, an expansive oak book shelf beside it. A Victorian style couch and an old-timey radio in front of the window where filtered light snuck its way through lace curtains.

"All right, fella. We sleep upstairs. The kitchen and bathroom are down the hall. The den is off the kitchen. Nothing in there much looking at either, though I do have a nice flat screen to watch the games when fall comes."

"The games?"

"Hell yeah, son. College football. Hook em horns'. Got to watch something to stay sane around here when the temperature drops, plus it reminds me of home."

Rand nodded.

"Okay, we can go over all that later, but now it's time to get to business."

The man walked to the grandfather clock, opened its tiny door, moved the big hand to 7, the little hand to 3, then removed an ancient-looking hardbound copy of "The Woman in White" by Wilkie Collins from the bookshelf. Rand heard a click. The bookshelf swung opened slightly, the faint smell of trapped air drifting out. The Eagle slipped his hand inside it. Opened it all the way. A light emanated.

"Follow me."

Rand saw the man start down a flight of narrow, very steep, stairs. Felt a slight well of apprehension. Stood at the top, eyeing the steps nervously. Fear of being trapped? Fear of decension? Flashbacks to The Cavern? He couldn't place it. Watched the head below bobbing one step at a time.

"You okay, Phoenix? Don't tell me they sent a claustrophobic," the man shouted, not even looking back at him.

"No, I'm fine."

"Then, get moving. The door will close automatically behind you. Trust me, it is a lot roomier down here than it looks."

CHAPTER THIRTY

Rand had seen a HAM radio before, had written an article at the newspaper on a local HAM radio club. Still recalled the giddiness of the club members, eager to talk about the oblong black boxes with their blinking dials and the slick black microphones.

But, this was different. This unit was much older.

Chunky knobs and oversized dials faced out on a slate gray metal box. A black and red tuner ran across the top of the unit, tiny numbers and symbols adorning its surface. A speaker sat to the right of it, looking like it had been yanked from a 1970s stereo. To the left of the unit was a faded gray microphone.

"Wow," Rand said. "That must weigh 20 pounds."

"More like 30," the man said. "But I prefer quality and, while the newer models might have more bells and whistles, this model has never let me down yet. Sturdy and reliable. I'll take that over sexy any time. Close to perfect as you can get."

The radio belonged in yesteryear as did everything else in the cellar. A sagging bookcase sat in the corner, its shelves crammed with notebooks and manuals, loose papers bulging out in a haphazard pattern. On top of the bookcase, sat a bottle of brown liquor. Two dusty glasses beside it. In the opposite corner was a gun safe. Black.

And in between these items sat Rand and the man. The Eagle. Both on opposite sides of an old card table, the HAM radio between them, Rand's backpack at his feet. The man had taken off his cowboy hat and revealed a thicket of salt and pepper hair. The man pushed a large black button on the radio. A warm red light blinked on and the sound of electricity purred in the room.

"All right, this may take a while to find a signal, so, go ahead and tell me what your SOP is," the man asked Rand.

"Pardon, me?"

"Standard operating procedure," the man eyed him warily.

"Uh, I really didn't have one…we had an emergency, our home, our base, whatever you call it was attacked, invaded. I made it out, took my backpack, like I was told, called, got directions, then got on a plane, landed here, used the phone and they told me to find The Eagle, then - "

"Stop, stop, stop. I don't need all the details, but you don't know what a SOP is? You must still be wet behind the ears. How long have you been with us?"

"It's hard to say, really…" Rand was at a loss for words. Mind whirring. Hands sweaty. Trying to piece everything together. Did he even commit to 'us'? Words interrupted his confusion.

"Son, I hate to pry. But who are you? We aren't ever supposed to talk about that, but only high priority cases get the code name The Phoenix. Hell, I've only had two in 40 or so years. You don't know what your standard operating procedure is once you establish contact. You look at my HAM radio like it is from outer space. You got this far, so you aren't completely out of your depth. I'm frankly puzzled. I apologize for being so blunt, but I have little left to lose at my age. You some hotshot young gun? Got in way too over your head too fast?"

Rand stared at the table. Cleared his throat. Spoke.

"Okay, if you want to do this, let's at least be fair. What's your name? Give me your story in five minutes. Then, I'll give you mine."

"You got a lot of balls sitting in my house, in my safe room, requesting information from me, you know that?"

Rand tensed. Dropped his eyes back to the table. Squeezed his hands shut and then open again. Felt the slight strain of muscle in his shoulder. An uncomfortable hush in the room. Took a deep breath. Lifted his eyes. The man's gaze met his, then the man eased back in his chair, the edges of his mouth slightly turned upward in a smile.

"But that's okay," the man broke the silence. "I like a man with a pair. Like I said, damn good people around here, but not many men drop their stones that quick. Your accent betrays your origins Southern boy, but, your actions tell me you might have a wild hair. So, yes, I will indulge you first. But on one condition. Don't bullshit me when it is your turn."

"Yes, sir."

"Okay," he had his hands behind his head. "I've got so many goddamn names, I don't even know who I am half the time anymore, but for the past 20 years or so, people just call me Winston. Winston Worsley. Like I said, I grew up in Texas, outside of Amarillo. Goofed off in high school, but still made good enough grades. Then I blew the damn roof off of my entrance exams for college. My principal saw something in me – you ever have someone like that? – anyway, he saw something, decided to fight for me to get a good education. I was goin' to go to some state college and then one day, I got an acceptance letter to Stanford of all places. Full ride. Stanford. I said, 'What the hell.' I like sunshine, California girls. So I went out there. Dicked around for a couple of semesters doin' my cowboy thing, chasing skirts, raising hell, fish out of water shit."

"Then I got to a class on computer programming of all things. Real early shit. But, there was more than that. There was a group of guys in that class who were into some far out stuff then. Creating codes. Code breaking. Not your average stuff, but different…Most of this was computer codes – real early, elementary shit - but sometimes we'd break out old World War II codes, amend them slightly, then see who could beat who. Then maybe take some Greek, translate it to German, translate it back to Greek, then create a cipher. Get it? Academic cock swinging, but I found it so damn interesting I couldn't stop. What's better? I was good at it. Okay, let me get to the meat of the story. Halfway through my sophomore year, I get paid a visit by a man named Eliot Waterstone. He was in his 60s, I guess. English accent, very refined. A gentleman if I ever did meet one. Said a company needed my help. Great pay. Great service to humanity. You know the drill, the old recruitment shit they give you," Rand had no idea, was lost at this point, but kept his mouth shut and listened. "So I bought in. This was, what – late 70s? We had the Cold War, computer technology was just starting, the oil crisis. But they put me right onto codes. I wanted to work with computers and that was the hot thing. Hell, even then, we knew it was the next thing, but they said, they needed someone in the field who could create codes, break codes, someone who could do things on the run. Do them fast. Improvise. I wanted to work on computers, but they wanted a code man, crazy huh? I mean real 19th century espionage. So I did it. Did the damn business for over 30 years. All over Europe. A little Asia. A little on the Pacific Rim, but mainly, Europe. West Germany. Berlin. I did all the spy stuff, but this company – you know us – with the power of the stones, we were light years ahead of the Soviets and the Americans. They were playing checkers, we were playing chess. And we played them against each other while we got what we wanted. I helped route more information on the Meridian in 20 years than just about anyone else in my zone. And, the bitch of it is, I liked it. I liked the creating, the misinformation, knowing the real inside game. I liked it all….then I met Lucy, the classic English rose. I realized then I wanted to get out. It was time to retire soon. To resign at least. To stop. Just to marry her. Take her far away. Take myself far away. Leave it all behind. All that would've been nice, but then the split happened and –"

The radio crackled to life: "Eagle, this is Kingfisher One. Eagle, this is Kingfisher One. Is Phoenix with you? Do you have the package? Copy?"

"Yep. I got the parcel….Strange cookies," he glanced at Rand, "But, I got it. What's next?"

"Location 67. Travel together. Destroy current location upon departure. Copy?"

"Yeah, I got you loud and clear."

"When you arrive at location 67, contact us."

"Yep, when?"

"Arrive at destination by 9 p.m. today."

"Gotcha, I know the drill."

"Hey –" Rand interjected, "Ask him if he knows anything about Hope?"

The man named Winston cupped his hand over the microphone shot Rand a deadly stare. Mouthed 'shut up.'

"Sorry about that Kingfisher One. Got some weather here, tossing off the satellite bounce I reckon. Infrequent communication channel. Talk to you soon. Out."

CHAPTER THIRTY-ONE

"What the hell was that son? We were on a coded call! Then Hope? You said Hope? What the hell is Hope?"

"Sorry. She was, well, is the only one I know. The only person I can trust anymore. I…I…Well, you can't imagine what we've been through together."

"I can imagine a lot more than you can, son. And I've been through it all," Winston stood blowing out his breath, running his hand through his hair again, standing and reaching for the bottle on top of the bookshelf.

"You know the headquarters in Austria?" Rand blurted.

Winston froze in motion. Turned slowly. Arm dropping back to his side. Eyed Rand.

"What do you know about the headquarters in Austria, son?"

"Yeah, I know about them or what was them. I – we – destroyed it. It's gone. Nothing but a crater in the ground."

He looked at Rand in shock. Then almost quizzically. Reached back to grab the bottle, pulled it down along with two dusty glasses. The man sat. Poured a finger's worth of whiskey into each glass. Slid one over to Rand.

"All right now, Phoenix. You've heard enough of my story. Tell me yours. I have a feeling I might need this," he lifted this glass in a silent toast.

"I don't drink liquor."

"No problem, chief" he said as he grabbed Rand's glass, tilted it and consumed in a single swallow. "Ah, just the stuff. Now, get started."

"Here's the Cliff Notes version. My grandfather left me a map to destroy. I got chased. I got kidnapped. I was taken to The Castle. They found some of the Meridian through the map, then –"

"Slow down. Slow down. Slow down. Damn son." Winston lifted a hand to his temple, closed his eyes. "Okay, start over. Your grandfather? What was his name?"

Rand hesitated.

"Come on. I'm all you got to trust right now. Are you just going to sit there like a stubborn mule all night? Shit, I've got a couple of guns down here. You want them as insurance? Would that make you feel better talking to me?" The man gave a chuckle. "I'm too old for this. Kidnapped? Chased? Austria? Just start over. Slowly. Who was your grandfather?"

"Henry O'Neal."

The man sat there staring at Rand. His eyes slowly moving over his face. Studying him. Trying to peer into him, Rand thought, wanting to see if he was true. If his words were real.

"I'll be damned," a low whisper escaped from the man's throat.

"What? Did you know him?" Rand asked.

The man dropped his head, stared at the table. Twisted his lips in a look of resolve. Locked his eyes on Rand.

"So you'd be Andrew and Madeline's boy?"

"Yeah, that's right."

"Son of a bitch. Small world."

"What do you mean by that?"

"Looks like we have a lot of talking to do. How about this? We need to get out of here in about half an hour to make it on time. Help me pack. Load up and then we can play catch up on the way. Work for you?"

CHAPTER THIRTY-TWO

Winston walked to the gun safe. Twirled the knob. It opened. Rand saw two well-oiled AK-47s and a line of pistols hanging beside them.

"You know how to shoot?" Winston asked.

"Kind of."

"Shit. Kind of. Well, Mr. Kind Of. Help me with these."

He handed Rand one of the AK-47s, a Beretta 92F and a handful of magazines for each.

"These are not the latest on the market, but it's what I prefer and seeing that you didn't bring in any cutting-edge weaponry with you, I reckon this will work. We'll stuff these AKs in this gym bag. Tuck the Beretta in your waistband or wherever you want to keep it. Just keep the damn safety on or you'll blow off your leg."

"Yes sir."

"This should do it. If we need more than this, well, we're already up the creek by then, got it?"

"Yes sir." Rand was beginning to feel like he was back on the football field. Orders. Yes sirs. Action. Listen up. Finish the drill. "Quick question though."

"Yeah?"

"AK-47s? Aren't those a little...antiquated?"

"Hell, yes, they are. But they are easy. Let me ask you something, you ever seen any photographs of African War Lords with those God-forsaken child soldiers?"

Rand recalled the images. Chilling smiles from fresh faces. Barefoot, but armed.

"Yeah."

"Yeah, well what kind of gun did they all have?" Winston answered his own question. "Damn right, an AK-47. Easy to use. Easy to load. Never breaks. Got it?"

"Yes sir."

"Good, grab something to drink from the fridge if you want, but make it snappy. I'm going upstairs to pack. I'll meet you at the truck in 15."

CHAPTER
THIRTY-THREE

The truck made a left out of the driveway and headed south. Rand's Beretta lay in his lap. The gym bags in the backseat along with their backpacks. Winston began humming some old country tune Rand couldn't place.

"Aren't you going to destroy that, uh, your house?"

"Hell no. After all I've sacrificed over the years? I love that house. My Lucy died there. I can still smell her perfume when I walk through it. I'm not going to blow it up. Destroy current location they said. Hell no. They can kiss my ass. Shoot, old Osborne down the road will take care of my livestock. I called him before we left. The house will be just fine whether I come back or not. I'm going to let it be."

Rand nodded.

"So we're heading to Location 67? What exactly is that? And how do you keep up with these numbers?"

Winston dryly chuckled.

"One question at a time. Those coordinates are for a small cabin on Lake Telos, several hours south, southwest from here. It's only about two and a half hours away, but we're taking the back roads and then the back roads upon those roads. We want to stick to the old logging roads and other half-forgotten roads. And, yeah, I've got it all memorized, so no GPS tracking. No cell phone. Nothing. Just two lonely hunters driving through the dusk, get it?"

"Yes, sir."

"And about the numbers? It is not really as hard as it seems. I've got a finite number of things I have to keep up with that I don't write down – things like codes, locations, etc. As long as I know those, it's easy. If it's a critical job, someone brings me all the information I need. But I haven't had a serious job in years. Right now, I memorize just the basics: Phoenix equals highly sensitive package or person. Location 67 equals a cabin at Lake Telos. 56 equals a motel room in Van Buren, Canada, about 10 minutes over the border. Kingfisher One is the main contact, the prime mover over here, in North America. Kingfisher Two is Europe. I got about five other codes and names I keep up with, but they don't mean anything right now. Understand?"

"I think so."

"Trust me, it's not that hard. It was a shitload harder when I was working in Berlin."

Rand peer through the window, grimy with dust and the skeletons of bugs. The Maine dusk was descending. They crested a rise. Below, Rand saw a colossal forest of evergreens spread out like a carpet.

"Good Lord," he exclaimed.

"Yeah, gorgeous isn't it? Like I said back roads upon back roads. This is as close as you can get to real wilderness in the Lower 48. You ever seen so many Christmas trees? Enjoy the ride, uh, Phoenix, but wait a second, I never got your name. What is your first name?"

"Rand."

"Rand. Rand O'Neal. That'll work. We can drop the code names now. Rand. Good strong name. Of course, your dad always did have a penchant for good names. And I mean all names. Names for jobs. Names for even a basic code. He would play around with the vernacular just to suit the situation."

"So, you knew him? You really knew him?"

Rand waited. Winston stiffened. Glanced in the rear view mirror. Coughed.

"Yeah, I knew him. Worked with him for about seven, eight years. Him and your mom. Only met them face to face a few times. I was more logistical support, behind-the-scenes like I said. I created the codes, but they used them. Put them into real action. They were the real deal, the real operatives out in the field. Behind enemy lines….back when there was only one real enemy…before we realized the enemy half the time was ourselves… back before the split….." His voice drifted off and he glanced into the rear view mirror again.

"You mind grabbin' me a cigarette from that pack in the glove box?" He asked.

Rand opened the glove box. Found a pack of Marlboro Reds. Handed them over to Winston who shook one out. Offered the pack to Rand.

"Ah," he hesitated. "No thanks, I quit."

Winston nodded. Stuffed the pack inside his shirt pocket. Flicked open a lighter and opened his window a crack. The plumes of blue smoke wisped out and drifted behind them. Rand could feel the tension in the air. Knew the man didn't want to talk about his parents. But, Rand couldn't let it rest.

"You know, I was ten when they died."

"Yeah," Winston took another drag, blew out a long line of smoke, ran his hands along the steering wheel. "I did the math…. figured as much."

"Yeah, I knew them, but I didn't really know them…you know, like I wanted to."

"Yeah…sorry son, I didn't know them much either. Like I said, I mainly worked behind the scenes. I met your folks a few times during debriefings or when they returned from some mission and we needed to talk face to face…well, I guess you want details, huh?" Winston didn't wait for a response, just shifted in his seat. "Well, your dad, like I said was brilliant. Sharp as a damn tack. But he also had a sense of humor. I mean some of the code names he used or ciphers he concocted were funny as hell. He named one mission after a woman who worked in the Austrian Embassy who was a looker, I mean she was foxy. So we had to extract her and he named the mission something like Hot Trot or Behind Enemy Thighs. Of course, only a few of us got it, but it was funny as hell. Great sense of humor. And that's not something you run into a lot with our group, so I appreciated that. He stood out like that. In a good way. Had drinks with him once…yeah, can't remember, exactly. Late 70s? Early 80s? London? Not important. Just him and I went out for a couple of pints at a dump of a pub. Had a great night. Nothing crazy, just good laughs. Your mom? Can't remember much, son. Met her once or twice. Sorry. She was a beautiful woman, though, I remember that and I say that with no disrespect. She was a true lady…they were quite a pair together. Does that help?"

Rand felt himself smiling in the growing darkness, their faces faintly lit by the green LED lights emanating from the car's clock radio.

"Yeah," he said softly. "Thanks. Anything helps."

The truck rumbled along. No headlights or tail lights in sight.

"Question," Rand said.

"Yeah?"

"So we get to this lake and this cabin. Is that like another outpost or whatever? What's the deal?"

"No outpost. Just a cabin out in the middle of nowhere. From what I reckon we're going to Lux next."

"Lux?"

"Shit, sorry. I forgot you are new. Yeah, Lux. Lux Engineering. Our main North American headquarters. The real deal. Not an out-lier like me or that hole in Alabama. But the brains of the operation."

"Where is it?"

"You ever been out west, son?"

CHAPTER
THIRTY-FOUR

"Wake up. We're almost there."

Rand felt a firm hand shaking his shoulder. Eyelids sticky. His mouth was dry. Had been asleep too long. The rattling hum of the airplane an atonal drone or an out-of-tune nursery rhyme had soothed him to sleep after leaving Maine. He sat up in his seat, the blanket he had been using as a pillow crumpled into his lap. Rand half-folded it, set it on the floor in front of him.

His lower back was stiff. He and Winston had been picked up that morning at Lake Telos after a fitful night of sleep on a sofa followed up by a cold breakfast of canned pork and beans and instant coffee. A tri-phibian plane had circled over twice then glided like a heron onto the lake's steely surface, water flashing from under its skis as it coasted to their dock. Rand found the plane amazing for its multi-purpose uses, but discovered its comfort was lacking. Not that he had any reason to complain, but after the plush cabin of the Lear, the utilitarian plastic seats and bare floor weren't exactly first-class worthy.

"Take a look," Winston said.

He was leaning over his seat and pointing to the window. Rand blinked his eyes, trying to wake. He stared out the window to the washed out sky and then below to the land rising to meet them.

Tan.

Everything seemed tan.

Then he noticed the subtleties. The browns, the beiges, patches of sienna running like a rivulet before dying out, occasionally, a wash of sand and the scattered burnt green of stunted desert shrubs.

A series of hills and small mountains interrupted the seemingly endless flatlands. Or were those mesas? Then they disappeared and the view surrendered to the flatlands.

"How do you like the desert, son?"

"Gorgeous…in a vacant kind of way."

"Vacant?"

"Yeah, I mean, I find it beautiful, because it is so…clean. Open. So devoid of anything. Just rock, sand, shrub, brush. No houses, highways, McSubdivisions, trash."

"Yeah, I here you. There is a certain type of serenity when man decides not to muck things up."

The pilot's voice crackled through the speakers.

"Hang tight crew. We're preparing for descent. Make sure you're buckled up."

Rand reached to buckle his belt, realized he never had unlocked it. Winston laughed.

"Yeah, that's right. You've been sewn up the whole time, son. Hell, you didn't even budge when we stopped for fuel in St. Louis. You were out like a light."

"What did I miss?"

"Not much. Just about 8 or so hours of flight. No excitement. Maybe one rain storm. Rare turbulence. That's it."

"Any word from anybody on anything?"

"Nothing. Which is good, by the way. Smooth sailing, or rather, flying."

"What time is it?"

"Three in the afternoon. Hottest time of the day out here."

Rand nodded. Felt the plane begin to descend. Forced a yawn. Ears popped. The tans outside the window growing closer. Felt his stomach drop.

Then the bump of wheel against runway.

CHAPTER
THIRTY-FIVE

The heat was not oppressive like the humidity-laced South-ern heat, but was dry and burning. And everything was bright, light lancing off of everything, the faded grey run-way, the desert, the plane.

Winston was steering them in a golf cart toward a towering stone wall split by two iron doors. Behind them, at the opposite end of the runway was a cluster of gleaming silver structures, each one several stories high and the length of four football fields. Industrial facade. No windows. An abundance of reflecting metal. The most dominant building had the words, 'LUX Engineering' emblazoned in a royal blue.

"So, what's what? Is this all, the, uh, headquarters?" Rand asked.

"On that end is our business. Lux Engineering. Aerospace tech-nology. It's been operational since the 70s. It's a solid, middle-of-the-road manufacturer of small parts for Lockheed Martin and Boeing. They, well, we, do everything. It used to be valves and seals, but, now it's more about electronic sensors primarily in the engine area – without getting too technical."

"I'm confused? A business? Strange cover isn't it?"

"Hell, great cover. Hide in plain sight. We've got a legitimate company here. Best cover there is. It's in the desert – which makes sense – so there is a lot of air space for testing, plus we stay just under the radar enough to make a little money, but not get noticed for big contracts. We also don't have any lobbyists in Washington angling for deals or funding from the military-industrial complex. Like I said, just a small player in the giant aircraft game."

"But, what came first? You said the headquarters was here. Did it build around this or did the company start afterwards?"

"One in the same, you might say. We started with a base out here, in the middle of nowhere in the 1970s, before the split. A group of us were already pre-empting you might say. We'd been piddling around North America for too long, small offices in New York and San Francisco. But, we knew that would be easy. Too easy to find. So we moved out here. Started our base operations over there," Winston pointed to the wall they were approaching. "There was an abandoned town out here. There had been some government military testing in the 1950s. There was no radioactive fallout, but the residents were sketchy and took a quasi-corporate buyout from us to leave. We bought the town and restored some of the buildings. Eventually we needed better access to food, transportation and such, so we started Lux Engineering, built our own campus and razed all the old buildings, except for The Library. With Lux up and running, we were able to get the access we needed to transportation and supplies and we didn't have to house everything in what was left of the town. Now we've got the plant and a decent campus with good housing, cafeteria, gym, you name it. Plus we're in Harding County. You ever heard of that?"

"No, sir."

"Damn right. Smallest county in New Mexico. Roughly 700 people in the whole county."

Winston stopped the golf cart in front of the doors.

"This," Rand said, pointing to the wall that loomed over them, "is a little much isn't it? What is this – like 16 feet high, or something? I mean, where's the moat and crocodiles? Do you have any archers on top?"

Winston sighed.

"You are a smart ass, aren't you? Damn. It's not for protection, son, but for noise reduction when they do any testing on the runway."

The doors leisurely opened and a tall, willowy woman, her skin the color of cinnamon glided out, braids of silver hair dangling regally down her neck. She wore a long silk dress, the hue of a pale morning sky. Despite the heat, a royal blue shawl adorned her shoulders.

"My friend," she said in a melodious voice. A voice as serene as the patter of raindrops, but also with a strength of thunderclaps, Rand thought.

"Mary, it's been a long time," Winston said and tipped his cowboy hat.

She smiled. "Yes," then peered at Rand with the most amazing eyes Rand had ever seen. Almost grey, but with a blue sheen. And they seemed born from of a regal, yet, peaceful place.

"Ma'am," Rand said, a slight bow at the waist, though he did not know why.

No hand was extended, only a smile. "Hello Rand. My name is Mary Celest. Winston and I worked together many moons ago."

"Beggin' your pardon, Mary," Winston interjected. "Don't let her kind voice fool you Rand, we worked together, but she did the real work with the stones."

A melodious, lilting laugh.

"Oh, Winston, you know we're too old of friends to stand on such formality. Come in out of this sun. You look a bit tired and I might know the right tonic. How about a drink?"

"There is nothing I would love more. But I've got to get him to The Operatus first."

She nodded. "Of course, you must. But, afterwards, you will meet me? I'll have a bottle of wine for us."

"Sure. Bar in the same place?"

"Yes. Though now they call it The Café. Things have become a bit more refined since the last time you were here."

"What a coincidence. Just like me."

CHAPTER THIRTY-SIX

I f Frank Lloyd Wright designed a college campus, Rand imagined this is how it would look. Five buildings all in a similar style separated apart from each other to form a crescent. All the buildings had a prominence of glass and bleached brown stone unearthed from the desert. Low slung roofs. Absurdly long rectangular windows. Doors, window frames and pillars a muted nickel.

Even though each structure was a few stories high, the elongated foundations gave them the appearance of rising from the earth like a series of planned mesas.

The buildings were connected with a series of paths constructed of white pebbles. Between the paths were rock gardens, a few flowing fountains and even a handful of tended vegetable gardens sprouting a variety of peppers, pumpkins, tomatoes and sweet potatoes, wild bursts of lush purple and angry red and ripe orange, a stark bloom of color against the duo-tone landscape.

"This is the campus," Winston said, slightly ahead of Rand as they wound through the buildings. "You've got two dorms, a cafeteria and bar, a gym and research center, unless they changed all that since I was last here."

"And when were you last here?"

"Hell. I don't know. A few months after I buried Lucy. Maybe, what, six years ago. Thought that would be my last trip."

They walked in silence, the crunch of their boots on the gravel.

"This is impressive," Rand said. "So, who actually lives here? Are they all employees of Lux or people who work with us?"

"It's a mix. Half work for us and about half work for Lux. Some of the Lux families live in a small subdivision about eight or so miles from here. They've got a filling station out there, but that is about it. The other Lux employees live here with us. But, they have their own dorm and tend to keep to themselves. We just tell them, regulars, as we call them, that we work on top secret stuff. High Intelligence. Tell them the less they know the better. It works out. Anyway, you can get the tour later, but I need a drink and you need to see The Operatus."

"Did you say The Apparatus?" Rand asked. "What, is that a computer? Artificial Intelligence? I don't want to be hooked up to a machine. I don't even trust cell phones."

"No, not Apparatus. I said, 'Operatus.' Latin. Damn, I can't believe your grandfather let you skip Latin," Winston shook his head.

"Hell, some days my grandfather was just glad I graduated high school."

A chuckle, then, "Okay, The Operatus. It means The Operative. The man in charge you might say. I'm taking you to Waterstone. Eliot Waterstone."

"So, he lives in one of these buildings?"

Winston chuckled. "No, son. He would not tolerate such…what he would call unnecessary comforts as this. He actually lives in what's left of the town - The Library."

CHAPTER
THIRTY-SEVEN

P alm fronds cast shadows of half-moons, scimitars and curved smiles across the path which was occasionally scuffed by Winston's boots that kicked up dust.

They had walked past the last of the campus buildings onto the palm-shaded trail which led to The Library roughly a quarter of a mile away.

Rand caught glimpses of the town's former buildings, old slabs of concrete still pushing out from the desert floor, like chipped teeth, the occasional glimpse of a sidewalk covered in sand.

At the end of the trail loomed The Library. Though it had been bitten by wind and sun, it still retained dignity. Built from tan bricks, it stood like a lone sentry in the desert. Arched windows pierced its otherwise stoic facade. At the rear of the building, a modest cupola rose, the desert light winking off the window panes. The duo arrived and Winston paused at the bottom of a small flight of steps that led to an arched portico under four Doric columns.

"Rand," Winston placed a hand on his shoulder, startling him. "This might be a little odd for you."

"Odd?" Rand gave a dry laugh. "Have you forgotten everything I've been through lately? Odd? Come on Winston. Give me a break. Everything is odd."

Winston looked him in the eye. Hard. Bold.

"Let me put it this way. I don't mean odd like a bad thing. Just

different...Waterstone....he's old. He sees things...differently...
He's brittle, but brilliant. You might beat him in a fist fight, but in
a battle of the minds, he would tear you up...and like I said, he's
old. He's been with us, well, as long as I can remember."

"How old?"

"Hell, probably somewhere around 120 or so. Been working in
one way or the other with The Slendoc Meridian for probably 90
years."

"90 years?"

"You got it. I told you. He's old as dirt. And thank God he's on
our side."

CHAPTER
THIRTY-EIGHT

A huge iron ring protruded from the frowning visage of a daunting iron door, almost daring Rand to knock.

Rand gave a light tap of his knuckles on the door. Stood still. Waited. Crossing his right hand over his left wrist, an old technique of respect his grandfather had taught him.

"You might not want to stand out here waiting," Winston said. "He's expecting you, so go ahead. He's in the back of the building. You can't miss him. No one else is in there. This is where I leave you now. Find me later and I might even buy you a drink."

"You aren't coming with me?"

"Wasn't summoned," Winston said matter-of-factly. He tipped his hat. Winked.

"Well, here we go again," Rand said.

He entered, closed the door gingerly behind him.

The musty smell of old books filled the air. Dusty shafts of sunlight poured in from arched windows, their rays broken up by rows upon rows of bookshelves, where books lay haphazardly. Some upright, standing attention in order. Others on their side, splayed half-open.

A marble aisle ran between the bookshelves, enclosed with roughhewn bricks, each one displaying indecipherable symbols and characters. Strange, yet familiar, to Rand. He wanted to pause, to study them, but felt impelled to meet Waterstone. He urged himself ahead, boots on the floor. Click clack. Click clack.

The distant hum of an air-conditioning unit coming to life. A welcome push of cold air from above. A shiver ran across Rand's chest, the perspiration lifting off his skin, the coolth of a salve to his sun-beaten brow. He ran his hand through his hair. Continued to walk. Cautiously. Not afraid, but intimidated. Did not want to be surprised.

Could hear nothing, but the gentle patter of the artificial breeze from the air conditioning rattling the pages of half-open books.

Ahead a gorgeous circle of light waited, dozens of rays from the cupola shooting down to illuminate a circle of marble, ringed with the same stones from the path.

In the middle was a symbol Rand recognized.

Jagged, cruel legs with a flat roof and a circle in the middle. He recognized it from the map his grandfather left him to destroy. Had seen it on the standing stones Kent said were Atlantean in The Cavern. What was it? What did it mean?

A raspy, but strong, voice called to him from the shadows somewhere beyond the light.

"Come in, come in, into the light." Rand could clearly detect an English accent. Not harsh, like Cockney. Not erudite like Kent's. But gentle. Soft? No. Weak? No. Peaceful, but with vigor to it. "Please, do not be afraid of the dark, my child. I am only old and direct light gives me tremendous headaches, but there is nothing to fear here."

Rand stepped into the circle of light, its luminosity fierce and vibrant.

"Ah stop. Just there. Just for a moment, let me see," a distinct eagerness in the voice. "I want to see you in the light. I want to see who you've become or, rather, who you are. The seed of The O'Neals."

As the voice spoke, a figure emerged from the shadows. A tall wispy man whose carriage was held up by a silver cane, the handle of it in the shape of a greyhound. The man's body was not bony, but thin, whispy, almost like a wraith. He walked forward, one hand on the cane, the other held above his head as if he was shielding off a drizzle of rain or fending off the sun. He was dressed in a pair of gray flannel trousers and had a white dress shirt tucked in. All very neatly ironed and crisp and out of place for the desert.

"Excuse my slowness, my body does not respond to my mind like it used to. It is such a betrayal. We grow old and our trousers are rolled and our bodies rebel. I feel like an ancient turtle," a depreciating chuckle.

The full face moved from the shadows and into the half-light. Dark brown eyes behind a pair of round tortoise shelled glasses. Tall brow. Slate grey hair swept back into neat, though thinning rows. Aquiline nose. High cheekbones. A once strong jaw. The wrinkles around the mouth were deep, but not menacing. Serious, but not threatening. Rand immediately sensed a tenacity and, yet, something of great sadness that seemed to hang about the man, like an invisible coat.

"Ah, I see." The eyes stared into his. Again, the eyes. Deep brown like rich soil. Rand felt intimidated, but not scared. Intrigued, but not anxious. He stared back. The man gave a dry laugh. "I stare at you. You stare at me. But, ah, that is fair play, then, isn't it?" A lightness to the voice. The soft chuckle. Rand found himself smiling.

The man reached toward Rand's face. Froze in mid-air.

"May I?"

"Pardon, me?"

"May I touch your face? With my eyesight coming and going, I tend to rely on touch and sound more. If I could just touch your face, I could get a stronger sense – pun intended – of who you are."

"Sure, uh, yes sir."

The hand rose. In the full light, Rand could see the papery skin stretched over ancient bones. Brown kidney spots splotched on once white skin. Fingers long, elegant. The fingers of a pianist, Rand decided. He felt cold fingers move over his cheeks, a thumb grazed gently over his eyes, his nose. The full palm against his cheek.

"Ah, I see. Your father and grandfather's hairline. The jaw of your mother no doubt, and probably her lips, too, though I won't touch them," again the soft chuckle. "That will do. Thank you, young O'Neal."

The hand dropped. Rand's face slightly cool from the fingers. "Sir?"

"I can read a lot in the lines of a man's face, but my apologies, we haven't been properly introduced. I believe they told you my name. I am Eliot Waterstone. And you are Rand O'Neal. And we meet at last. You may call me whatever suits you. I have been called many things. I do like Eliot though. It makes me feel young again. Does that sound too sentimental? For years they called me Waterstone or The Kestrel. But all so formal, so discreet and I need no excess dignity now, no need for code names. May I call you, Rand?"

"Yes, sir."

"Good, good. A good strong name. Now, please come sit down over here. It is dark in the corner, I know, but we have some light. Forgive my lack of creature comforts, but all I really need is a soft place to sit, a bed for a rare bit of sleep, a bit of light to read and tea. So, please make yourself comfortable."

Rand followed the shuffling figure out of the circle of light and toward a half-darkness, smudged with blurred shapes and odd shadows. He blinked. Held his eyes closed. Opened them. Hoping to adjust. A line of sconces jutting from the wall poured soft light onto the ceiling. As the light shifted, Rand saw a low round table in a corner flanked by wing-backed chairs.

And the walls. The walls were covered in writing. Long, elegant cursive lines, interspersed with the occasional measurements or diagrams. Rand peered closer. Saw some of the letters were in English, French, Latin and, there they were again, the strange symbols and characters. Symbols he had seen on the map from his grandfather. Symbols he had seen on the standing stones in The Cavern. In the center of the wall hung a colossal map. It was constructed of a strange white material and had drawings of what appeared to be continents, oceans and islands. Symbols, numbers and half scrawls dotted its surface.

CHAPTER
THIRTY-NINE

"Your interest is drawn to the map, I see?" Eliot had paused a few feet ahead. Stopped. Turned. Looked Rand in the eye.

"Yes. Yes, sir."

"Most are the first time they see it. There will be time to discuss that later if you wish, but, now let us sit and talk if we may."

Rand followed the shuffling footsteps to several stuffed chairs surrounding a round coffee table in the corner. On its surface lay several books. Old fat tomes, lush leather and bound by a lock. Newer slim paperbacks, cracked spine and dog-eared, a handful of scrolls. A few legal pads with dignified cursive writing and, to Rand's surprise, a silver laptop with an illuminated Apple symbol in the middle. An electric tea kettle and two cups on one end of the table. In the center, was a round bowl made of copper. Clear water swelled to its edges and a few tea lights sailed on its waves, the light they cast surprisingly strong, tossing the odd shadow play of water light on the ceiling.

"Please sit." Eliot motioned to an empty chair. "Tea?"

"Sure, I mean, yes sir."

Rand caught a glimpse of a smile on the face, half-hidden in the shadows.

"Always the manners, your family. I always appreciated that. Most of us here have manners. We are not a barbaric sort. At least I hope not, but, that does not mean one cannot appreciate good taste, respect and gentility…and of course class does not create culture as money does not create nobility…Ah, I digress again… Here, here, I have an electric kettle here. Could you do the honors of heating it up and pouring us two cups? A bit of honey for me and for you if you like gifts from the prince of flight. Sorry, I have no biscuits, but we can manage. Of course, it is probably too warm for you to drink hot tea, but you can let it cool."

Rand switched on the kettle and the low rumbling began. Eliot's hands placed together under his chin.

"So, how is Winston? Same old cowboy?"

"Yes sir." Rand gave a small laugh. "He's fine, though. Took care of me."

"Good. His unique personality was always a welcome addition to so many of the stuffed shirts around us."

The sound of boiling water. The click on the tea kettle echoed like a gunshot across the silence of the room. Rand automatically rose, grabbed the kettle and poured them both two cups.

"Ah, thank you, my boy. You can never have too much tea. What is it? A cup of tea and a book too big, there is no such thing?"

"I think you have that a bit backwards, but that is how it goes. A C.S. Lewis saying."

"Yes. Yes. But then, what did Wilde say? 'Talent borrows, Genius steals.'"

CHAPTER FORTY

A n awkward hush fell between them before Eliot's voice pierced the silence.

"Rand, can we cut to the chase as the saying goes?"

"Ah, yes sir. Whatever we - you, I, need to do."

Rand had to will himself to slow his speech down. He found himself oddly eager. Eager to impress this man. Although, he had just met him, he wanted to gain his respect.

Eliot took a deep sip of tea, a tiny smile on his face.

"Rand, I know our location in Alabama was compromised. You, the team, the entire Mentone outpost. From what I have gathered -"

"Do you know if there were any survivors?" Rand knew he had cut the man off, butted in, but his lust for information on Hope bucked his reserve.

Eliot's head tilted toward the floor. He blew out a wispy breath, then raised his head. Looked into Rand's eyes.

"We are still waiting. Waiting for word to come in. But, not now, we haven't heard anything now. No beacons have sounded off. The phones are silent. All our drop spots and safe houses show no signs of contact. The HAM radio frequencies are quiet. Even the old rendezvous points. Nothing. You're the only one and I am sorry. I understand you were friends with them, especially one, in particular."

He had been efficient at shutting Hope out of his thoughts. It was easy when he was running for his life. There was no time to think about her, but, now the burst of her smile, the curve of her neck, the echo of her laugh flashed through his mind. He focused. Compartmentalize, he told himself. Willed his mind shut. Focused on the cup in his hand. The tea teasing the edge of the cup, a pool primed for descension.

"Rand, I am sorry about what happened there and I take responsibility. We have discovered as you did that Declan was a rather bad addition to our team. We vetted him, but he was rushed through the system too fast. Flaws overlooked. We lost most of our technology department during an incident last year in The Pacific Ocean. So we were in a rush. Thought we had to get someone in as soon as possible. All of this reliance on technology. People thinking we have to have it. And have it now. Now. Now. Now. We are losing our ability for patience, our ability to wait. And now we see what happens when we rush. Sometimes it is better to sit still and let things happen. To let things come to you, than to rush. We made a mistake bringing him on board. And, I am sorry."

"Yes, sir, me too," was all Rand could muster.

CHAPTER
FORTY-ONE

Eliot had ceased talking, perhaps to wait on something. Rand thought he could hear a faint hum somewhere beneath them, a slight vibration under the floor. He lifted the cup of tea to his lips, took a sip of the Earl Grey, a reminder of sharing a kettle with his grandfather when the two would return from a winter hike. The taste gave him a sense of peaceful nostalgia which he reveled in for a moment. Closed his eyes. Tried to relax his shoulders. Eliot cleared his throat.

"I want to talk to you about Austria, and about you and us and what's next. I hate to be so direct, but we have a rare advantage, though time is not on our side. May I?"

"Yes, sir," Rand said.

"I read in the last dispatch we received from Mentone that you had some misgivings about joining us. I assume you made up your mind to join us since you met Winston and accompanied him here. Am I right?" Eliot paused, thin lips blowing onto the surface of the tea, tiny ripples on its copper brown surface.

"Yes, I guess so. I, mean, I really haven't had much of a choice so far. I was thinking about it and then we got raided and everything went sideways. But, for now, I am. Can I say that? I mean, at least for now?"

"Yes, 'for now' works. I am pleased by it. The last many generations of your family have been a significant part of what we do. Of course, if you eventually decline or decide to leave, I would not harbor any ill will. You have to choose your own path. All that said, it is time for you to learn more about us. Our past. Our present and, most importantly, our future."

Rand had flashbacks to Kent's smug lectures in The Cavern, felt the angst rise in his heart. But it was a different type of angst. He wanted to impress this man. To be accepted by him. With Kent, it was a sheer respect he wanted born of force and danger. With Eliot, he wanted to be accepted for who he was.

"I imagine Kent told you plenty during your stay at The Castle," Eliot said. "Filled your head with everything, probably overwhelmed you. Belittled you and your family."

"My family," Rand scoffed. "I'm so tired of hearing about my family. My grandfather the traitor. My parents dead. Sacrificed." Rand felt ashamed. Said too much, too fast. Let his emotions run away. "I'm sorry, sir, but I am just weary of hearing this shi -, er, stuff about people treating my grandfather like he was a damn saint."

Eliot held up a hand. Interjected.

"Pardon me, what did you say?" an edge to the calm voice. "Did you say your grandfather was a traitor?"

"Yes, a traitor," and then he felt his voice began to crack. "Weren't my parents killed with my grandfather knowing? And I –" and here his voice cracked. "Was kept alive as some sort of bargain?"

Rand had buried this question deep within him. A place he did not visit. A place where he kept his darkness secreted away. Didn't want to believe it was true. Not his grandfather. Not knowingly let his own son be slaughtered. And then for what? For the sake of his grandson? Nothing made sense when he heard it in Austria. It had not made sense in Mentone or Maine. It did not make sense now.

"Dear, dear Rand. What did they tell you there?" The voice was sympathetic. Rand thought he almost detected a wetness in the man's eye. "My dear boy. No. Your grandfather had no idea your parents were going to die. They did it to scare us. Scare us all from leaving, from the split. To snuff out the flame. It was shortly after their death that your grandfather left them."

"What?"

"Yes. What words did Kent poison you with? What lies and riddles did he tell you?"

Rand felt a well in his throat. A tease of a tear glimmering in the corner of his eye. A sense of redemption. Of relief. He wanted to shout for joy. He wanted to cry tears of relief. But, first, he wanted answers.

"Left? Left? I don't understand. But, the map? What about the map? And the way all the people in Austria said they knew him? I don't understand?"

Eliot's head dropped to his chest. A deep breath.

"It is complicated, Rand. He left after your parents died. I don't know how much of the details he ultimately knew, but he knew that they died at the hands of The Organization. He cut off ties, but he was so intertwined with that world, he couldn't just let go. He didn't come and join us, though God knows I tried. I visited your house several times. Always late at night. Always unannounced. I even met you once when you were 11 or so, bright-eyed, but even then with a brood about you, but I doubt you remember me…." The voice trailed off for a moment, "But, he would not join us. Nor them. He said he was done. With everyone. He left, but, he was never completely out. He had made promises, sworn oaths. He still worked with them, you might say, but not for them. He played his part, but wanted to stay alone. Solitary. No country. No king. I believe he just wanted to protect you, to keep you safe and out of all of this."

"But the map? What about the map? How did he get the map?" Rand's voice now, bordering on anger. Confusion and frustration raged in his mind.

"He had," Eliot started, then paused, a sip of tea. "He had been given the map by someone to keep. Who gave it to him is not important. But he was given it almost as a failsafe. A last resort. Given it to protect. We thought he had it, but were not sure. I did not press it with him. But he had it and yet, by oath, he could not destroy it. Yet, he did not want either The Organization or us to have it. He was in a strange spot. He did not want your grand-mother involved. So, he left it to you. For you to destroy. Which you did in a way after all."

CHAPTER
FORTY-TWO

R and had surrendered to silence after Eliot's revelations. Set the cup of tea down on the table, half of it sloshing out into the gold-rimmed saucer. Leaned back in his chair, his neck back against the cushion. Eyes staring toward the ceiling. Hands in fists. A part of him wanted to break down into tears, to release a joyous sob of relief that his grandfather had been vindicated. And another part of him wanted to follow his grandfather's lead. To leave this world of secrecy and stones, and passwords and pointed lies and half-truths in candlelight. And then there was the other part. A part he knew that was not healthy. But it was alluring. A chance for justice. For peace. And to end these emotions that raged in his head.

He wanted revenge.

He craned his neck over to Eliot who was studying him. The cup and saucer now on the table. His hands in his lap.

"Yes, Rand?"

"You said earlier, something about me being a part of what you do, right?"

"Yes."

"Well, what do you mean, exactly? How can I help you? I mean, to be honest, sir, I'm just a smart ass with an anger problem at times. I hated school. I don't do well with authority or organizations and all that. I mean, I think you've got the wrong guy."

"The past is irrelevant, Rand. You are talented, more than you like to admit. You cover your intelligence and your sadness over your parents' death by being clever, rather than using your talents to be brilliant. You would rather not try at all, than try and fail. There is an ease at being a reporter for three years at a newspaper and actively turning down promotions. Am I right?"

"Yes, sir." Rand hated to hear the words. Knew they were true. Had been told it by too many girlfriends in the past he had pushed away. Friends he had parted with. Professors and bosses he had argued with. "Well, then," Rand said. "Why am I here if I am so fu- ah, screwed up?"

"You are not screwed up as you said, my child. You are acceptable. You just need to embrace who you are. Use your talents. Be the best you can be every second of every day. We need that from you, Rand. You, your family, have a special gift. A unique disposition to the Slendoc Meridian. Very few can withstand its effects without going mad. It, this trait, tends to run in bloodlines and our lines are very thin. I have that trait, but, look at me, I am too bone dry to get back out in the field. There are so very, very few of us left on our side. But, you. You have that trait. You can withstand the power of the stones. And we need someone like that. We need you. Our time using the stones to make us stronger, to enlighten our species is over. It is time to destroy them. Forever. But first we must get to them. And you can do that."

CHAPTER
FORTY-THREE

Back into the pitiless desert sun with no shade for remorse. Eliot had begged Rand's pardon, was going to rest, he said. His bones were weary. And Rand gladly acquiesced. His mind was spinning. The knowledge. Too much. He had questions beyond questions, but could accept the wait. Needed to let his reeling mind settle. He had walked back on the shaded path and now stood in between the buildings, half-rooted to the stone path. Gazed about. Where to go? He must find Winston.

"You lost?"

Rand wheeled and was met with the gaze of a wiry man, a hair under six feet tall. His skin was olive, close-cropped black hair and brown eyes. A smile spread across his face as their eyes met.

"Oh yeah," he said. "You are definitely lost. You've got that look."

Rand thought he detected a tinge of an accent. Was it Spanish? Italian?

"What look?" Rand asked.

"Don't worry about it. We all have it when we first get here. First of all, let's get out of this sun. Come on, follow me," he started, then stopped. "Actually, where are you going?"

"Uh, I am," Rand hesitated, "looking for The Café?"

"Ah, a man after my own heart. I am heading there too."

"By the way, I'm Rand," a handshake extended and met.

"Nice to meet you, Rand. You can just call me Spota."

"Spota?"

"Yeah, as in you ain't spota be doin' that. You ain't spota say that. You ain't spota blow shit up like that. You know? I have many other names. Some good, some bad. Some people call me 'The Man' because I am basically the best at what I do. Some call me Clooney, because I am so handsome, but most people here just call me Spota."

Rand laughed. Needed it. Spota's levity was instantly contagious.

"Spota, it is, then."

"Good, now let's get out of this heat."

CHAPTER
FORTY-FOUR

Low lights. Sleek marble-top tables. Windowless. Soft acid jazz emanating from hidden speakers. Abstract artwork dotted the walls above plush sofas. Rand felt like he was back in Atlanta in one of the hip bars in the city's Midtown district. He had always preferred the city's scant Irish pubs, quiet, low lit and comfy in their Guinness-soaked floors, but had, on occasion, accompanied a young lady to one of the hip bars. Usually only to learn to tame his mouth at the over-compensation and name-dropping of the city's wanna-be socialites and young faux-elite.

He felt the same way now as he scanned the room. Guarded. Tongue in check. Tight-lipped. A handful of people were seated throughout The Café. Most of the men with crew-cuts, the women with tight bobs. Linen and cotton. White shirts and pants. Rand out of place in his hiking boots, wrinkled olive pants and dirty black T-shirt. Now, very aware, he was in need of a shower and a change.

"All right, my friend, here you are," Spota said. "You can sit wherever you want, but you look like a man who likes to sit at the bar. Anyway, nice to meet you. I've been summoned for a meeting in the back so maybe I'll catch you around."

"Yeah, uh, thanks, I appreciate it. Next time I'll buy you a drink."

"Sounds good."

Rand watched Spota strut through the room, arms swinging at his sides, chest thrust out, tossing out the occasional greeting accompanied by a laugh. He opened a door at the back of the room and disappeared into darkness.

"Something tells me you don't belong here." A voice behind him.

Rand turned and was met with the face of the bartender, staring at him. Safe behind the bar, hands polishing a glass, eyes unthreatening, but studious.

"Pardon me?" Rand said. Felt a surge of agitation. Of insecurity. A tightness in his muscles. One fist already clinched.

"I said, something tells me you don't belong here. Looking at your shirt. That looks like a red clay stain on your shoulder. Good old fashioned unhydrated iron oxides. Sorry if I startled you, I work here as a part-time geologist and we don't see that type of dirt around here very often."

Rand instantly relaxed. Dropped his shoulders. Nodded.

"Hey, sorry about that buddy. You seem a little high-strung. Can I get you a drink?"

"Yes, please. A drink. Make that two. And that's okay. I just haven't slept in a while."

"No problem. What'll you have?"

"I suppose there's no chance of you having any Guinness on tap?"

The bartender smiled.

"Damn, you bet there is. We don't go through it as fast as the American beers, but we always have a keg around. A special request from the top, I heard. Something about an homage to someone. O'Malley? O'Toole? No, that's not it. O'Neal! That's it. Anyway, I don't mean to bore you with all the history, but, we've got it. I'll pull you up a couple of pints right now."

CHAPTER
FORTY-FIVE

R and was gulping down his second pint. Sitting at the bar. The bartender had been summoned by a group of tipsy, yet adorable, women on the other end of the bar that were giggling about which type of drink to order. Rand clasped his hand around the pint. Felt its cool glass under his skin, half content in the liquid anesthetic of the stout calming the restlessness in his brain, his muscles less tensed, his parched throat enjoying the black gold. The buzz from the beer strangely strong, but then again he couldn't remember the last time he'd eaten. Didn't really care. Looked around the room again. Did not see Winston. Oh well, he thought, time for another pint. He glanced down at the bartender who was still enthralled talking with the ladies. Didn't want to interrupt. But, he was thirsty. Was debating between raising his finger or waiting, when the voice boomed from the back of the room.

"There he is!"

Rand turned. Winston. Standing in the door that Spota had just entered, a glass of red wine cradled in one hand, a half-smile on his creased face and his eyes directly on Rand.

"Come on back here and grab a bottle of the 74' Bordeaux. Hell, make that two bottles. And a couple more glasses, too."

The bartender had snapped out of his tete-a-tete and within

seconds had two wine bottles and a trio of glasses in front of Rand.

"You with the cowboy, then?" He asked quietly.

"Yes. Yes, I am."

"Well, that explains a lot. Have fun."

CHAPTER
FORTY-SIX

Rand had reluctantly ambled off of the barstool and followed Winston down a walnut walled hall where a door the color of newborn moss waited.

"How long you been in there, son?"

"Not long. Just long enough to have a couple of pints."

"Hell, you didn't ask for me? I told them to keep an eye out for you."

"No, I didn't ask for you. I asked for a drink. And, secondly, I guess your description didn't match my looks. You should have told them something about a rugged intellectual with the body of an Adonis and the face of a cologne model."

Winston guffawed.

"Good God, boy. You sure you only had two drinks? You sound like you're beyond self-delusion."

Rand gave a wry grin.

"So, what's the scoop Winston? Where are we going?"

"We've got a meeting. I want you to meet some of the team."

"A meeting with two bottles of wine? Sounds like my type of meeting."

Winston shook his head.

"Oh, boy. And I thought you were full of yourself when you didn't have a drink in you. This will be interesting if nothing else."

CHAPTER
FORTY-SEVEN

A dining table in the center of the room. A single candle burning brightly in a burnished copper holder. One bottle of wine on the table caught the flickering light and swallowed its tongue revealing an empty bottle.

Two sat at the table. Mary Celest, her serene stateliness as apparent here as it was in the open air. Back straight. Delicate smile beneath the luminescent eyes. Silver braids twinkling like ribbons.

"Welcome Rand. Please sit. Have a glass of wine. We'll be eating shortly." Her voice as pleasant as he remembered. "I want to introduce you to –"

"Spota?" Rand spouted, without even thinking.

Spota sat beside Mary, a grin on his face, the green sheen of a Heineken bottle in his hand. "Small world, isn't it?"

"This is strange," Rand said, then, pulling out a chair, murmured, "aren't I a master of the obvious."

"So you two have met?" Mary asked, a general inquisitiveness in her voice, bordering on concern.

"Yes, uh, we did meet. I needed directions here. We ran into each other, and, well, here we are," Rand offered.

"How serendipitous," she remarked.

Rand tumbled into a seat, a tinge of elation brought on by the Guinness.

"So, to what do I owe this meeting of such esteemed individuals?" He asked. "I thought I was just meeting Winston for a drink."

Mary Celest gave a wan smile.

"Well, let me first assure you this isn't our modus operandi. We usually meet in quite sterile environments, and we like to move cautiously and deliberately. If we make a move to cause a shift in power with creation or destruction, we like to be certain, to have nearly 100 percent accuracy in the outcome. But, distinct events have recently occurred that have prompted us to expedite a mission." She paused, took a small sip of wine. "Let me back up a few weeks if I may."

Rand nodded.

"The Organization's North American headquarters houses several significant pieces of The Slendoc Meridian. Pieces that have been plucked from across the continent the last 400 or so years. We had been working for months on a plan to infiltrate the structure and detonate several bombs to destroy the stones. We actually were only a month out when Austria occurred, then –"

"Wait, Austria occurred? You mean…"

"Yes, the destruction of The Castle, rather your destruction of The Castle. Then, when that happened our plans were altered."

"How?"

"In many ways. First, the destruction threw The Organization into complete disarray. No one had known that you were there outside of Kent's inner circle. So when the building inexplicably went up in flames, it was a complete shock to their other outposts. While The Castle was only their European headquarters, it was also where Kent resided. And when he perished, a great wealth of knowledge and plans perished with him. In the aftermath, they have slowly begun to put pieces together, but they are still out of sorts. They are confused. Bewildered. And confusion is always a prime time to strike another blow."

She let the words set in. Rand poured himself a glass of the wine.

"Okay," he said.

"And there is another factor that emerged at the same time."

"What's that?"

She looked around the table before her eyes settled back on Rand.

"Candidly, you. As Eliot told you, the number of people who can withstand the power of the Slendoc Meridian has diminished but, you, however, like your father and your grandfather can handle the stones with limited exposure without permanent damage. We have a mission. We had a team set to infiltrate their headquarters. To destroy it from the inside. Spota here is part of the team. We had others, but they had issues at the last moment. Jeremy Del Monico was injured, breaking his leg in a freak fall and Dr. Lightfoot had a stroke and is –"

"Wait, what?" Rand said. "Dr. Lightfoot?" Then the question turning into a statement tinged with expectation. "You said Dr. Lightfoot! Hope? And a stroke? How? Is she here? Eliot said everyone had disappeared, I –"

"Oh, no. I am sorry. I should have phrased that better. Dr. Lightfoot is Jefferson Lightfoot, Hope's great uncle. I'm sorry, someone should have told you that before. As Eliot told you, the ability to withstand the Meridian runs in families. Dr., well, Jefferson has that gift as did," she stumbled with her words, "rather, does Hope...He was planning to go on this mission, when he had a stroke. Then, you surfaced and, to be transparent, that is why we need you to take his place."

Rand was silent. Too much. Too quick. Not even Mary Celest's soft tone could blunt the edge of her words. The expectation of Hope being alive. A flicker of faith, then dissipation and deflation. Her whereabouts still unknown. Probably dead. A ramshackle of images flooded his brain. Hope's face. The flaccid wilt of a stroke victim he interviewed when he worked at the newspaper, the capitulation. The phrase, 'Running in families.' His father's smile. His grandfather's letter. He froze. Closed his eyes. Damn. Damn. Damn. Anger welling inside him.

"Rand," Mary asked. "Do you need a minute?"

He wanted to tough it out. But his walls were cracked. His will broken. Too much information in one day. Emotional restraint destroyed. Smashed.

"Yes, yes. I do."

CHAPTER
FORTY-EIGHT

A small cough, dry air pushing up through his lungs. Another sip of wine. Another drag on a cigarette.
"Thought you didn't smoke," Winston said.

"I don't," Rand replied, let the irony sit in the air, like the smoke that hung about them, lingering still in the desert air.

Rand had left the meeting with a bottle of wine and found a patio outside The Café. He was half-reclining under an umbrella, his back to the waning sun, watching sunburnt shadows thrown across the desert floor. Winston had followed him. Discreetly. Respectfully. Brought another bottle of wine along. Rand asked for a cigarette.

Winston had not said a word. Just sat, smoked and drank with him. The patio empty except for the two of them. No sign of Mary Celest or Spota. The heat on his back lessened. The last rays of the sun sunk behind the horizon and a few stars made their arrival in the crystalline sky. The heaviness of the heat of the day relenting. Rand's mind playing the images over and over like a broken recorder. This day. Too much. Tried to push it all away with the wine, the cigarettes. But, the reel in his head didn't cease, only slowed down.

"Well, son, you gonna be all right?" Winston finally asked.

"Yeah," Rand said. He was slurring. Didn't give a damn. "Yeah. You bet. Fit as a fucking fiddle."

"I don't want to sound like an old woman, but you aren't going to solve anything by sittin' out here all night drinking. This is mighty fine wine, but it won't solve any of your problems, just push them off for a while, blur the edges of your pain, but tomorrow they'll be right back and, if you don't slow down, a hell of a headache with them."

"Winston?"

"Yeah, Rand."

"Can I tell you something?"

"Yeah, son. I'm listening."

"You do sound like an old woman."

They both laughed, the laughter of the half-drunk sharing a secret joke that crossed the lines of humor and sorrow. A rare broad smile on Winston, Rand half-doubling over, using his free hand to steady himself from falling out of the chair.

"Seriously," Rand broke the revelry. "I know. I know. Damn it. I'll do whatever. I'm in. I'm with you. Them. Whoever. Shit, I got nothing else. And I'm sorry. I'm sorry, I broke down," welling in the throat, then he pushed the words out. "I…just. I just couldn't handle anymore right now. I'm not weak, damn it, but everything has been too much."

Winston walked over, put his hand on Rand's shoulder. Squeezed it.

"I know, son. I know. But things are about to change."

CHAPTER
FORTY-NINE

A bell was ringing somewhere in the distance. A church bell? A warning bell? Not bells for celebration.

Rand rolled over in a bed. Opened his eyes. Darkness. Fumbled for a lamp. Anything. Nothing.

Heard a door open, saw a sliver of light framing a figure against the blackness. The subtle click of a light switch. A warm light revealed a spartan room. At the door stood Winston. The cowboy hat still cocked on his head. A cup of coffee in his hand. He pressed another button near the light switch and a shade beside Rand's bed whined, slowly rolling to the top, letting in a wash of desert sunshine. Rand saw the cause of the noise. The bell was an alarm clock set beside his bed. He switched it off.

Rand closed his eyes, held up a hand. His head sore. His mouth dry. His body aching.

"Come on, Winston. Ouch. Damn."

"Up and at 'em, son. We got a busy day."

Rand turned his back to the window, looked around the room. Yes spartan, but clean. Sleek, even. One bed. One desk. One dresser. All in a light wood gloss. Nickel coated knobs.

"Did you bring anything with you? Like coffee or Tylenol?" Rand asked.

"No, I didn't. Hell, you should be thanking me. I let you sleep in until almost 10. They wanted you up at 7 at the latest."

Rand grunted.

"Come on. We'll get you coffeed up with breakfast. Go clean yourself up, though. You stink. I'll wait out here. Be quick though."

Rand stumbled into the bathroom. Felt like he had drank himself through the night and halfway into tomorrow. Showered. Teeth brushed. A stack of neatly folded clothes on the counter. All tan. Cargo pants. T-Shirts. Pair of desert boots.

"Come on, now," Winston bellowed through the door. "We're on a schedule."

CHAPTER FIFTY

Half a dozen sets of free weight sets were arrayed along one wall. Two whirring fans bolted to the ceiling. Lining another wall was a treadmill and stationary bike. The middle of the room was spacious and vacant, though Rand did note the floor was made of a bouncy type of padding.

The walls were painted alternately navy blue and bright red.

"What's with the colors," Rand asked. "Patriotic? I thought we didn't serve a country."

"Our psychology department picked these out," Winston said. "The boys upstairs say red is a reinforcer of traits such as concentration, aggression and strength. The navy blue is to serve as a counter balance since it is associated with intelligence and logic."

"You believe that works?"

"Son, I don't know if it works or not, but I know I will take any advantage any time I can get it, and I know the brains we have working here are some of the best in the field so, I take it as it is. It might be a placebo effect, but it is better than no effect at all."

Rand had eaten a breakfast custom tailored for maximum vitality, or so the dietitian had told him. Egg whites. Bananas. Yogurt. And then a 64 ounce smoothie, "complete with a mega vitamin and protein boost," she said. Her pale complexion and ruddy red hair did not inspire the picture of health to Rand. He had demanded a pot of coffee, which, after some coaxing from Winston was provided.

Winston had sat across from him in the cafeteria, sipping on a cup of his own coffee. Black, of course. Other people flitted in and out. Lab coats. Tan slacks. Military garb. Exercise gear.

Rand still desired some real food and more coffee, but had followed Winston to a gym located inside one of the buildings. In the corner, Spota was punching a speed bag, fists whirring in a disciplined rhythm.

"Spota," Winston called out.

Spota stopped. Caught the bag in mid-stride. Turned.

"Good morning, sir. And good morning to you too, Rand."

"Morning," Rand replied. If Spota held any of the events of the night before against him, he did not show it. There was no shade of judgment or misgiving in his eyes, only an earnestness.

"You two need to be each other's shadow as much as possible, understand?"

They both nodded.

"This comes down from Eliot. Rand, you've got a ton to learn in a little amount of time so Spota will be your guide. He can answer any questions, give you some physical tidbits and teach you all about explosives."

"Okay," Rand replied, a bit tentatively. The term 'physical skills' sounded intriguing, but not necessarily enthralling with the weight of wine still recessed in his head. Explosives though? That was not anything he was remotely curious about.

CHAPTER FIFTY-ONE

"So, this is him." A deep voice came from behind them. Rand turned and was met by a tall man with the complexion of dark coffee. He had long arms and legs with the build of a basketball player, a couple of inches taller than Rand. But, he wasn't skinny. Even though he was clothed in utilitarian tan cargo pants and T-shirt, Rand noticed the wiry muscles underneath his skin, ripples of tendon and muscle twisted over and across bone. He had bright, brown eyes. A two inch long goatee with sparks of grey mixed in. Rand knew the type. Could almost smell it on certain people. This man had the killer instinct.

Rand extended his hand. The man's hand snapped up to grip it. A firm grip and Rand felt the man's eyes bore into his. He stared at Rand deeply. Intently. Then abruptly dropped his hand. Took half a step back. Crossed his arms. Looked Rand up and down, then back to peering into his eyes.

"Good," he said, then looking at Winston. "He'll do."

"Glad to know I'll do," Rand muttered.

"Take it easy, son" Winston said. "This is John Rhodes. And Rhodes doesn't play games and he doesn't tread lightly. If he gives you the once over and gives you the thumbs up, you're good."

Rand nodded. Wanted to fish for a smart ass comment, but, knew he was in over his head and, unlike a few weeks ago in Austria, he was in over his head with a good group of guys. It reminded him of playing football. You had to bust your tail during tryouts. Out muscle, out think, out hustle everyone to make the cut. But once you made the team, you were in and you part of the team. And when you were a freshman, you shut up and listened to the Varsity players. That was how he felt now. He was out of his element, beyond his depth, but in good hands and he didn't mind shutting his mouth to learn. He told himself to shelve his smart ass comments and listen.

"All right, gentlemen, I'll leave you to it," Winston said, lifting the cup of coffee to his mouth. "Rhodes don't take it easy on him. I think he might just need a good ass whippin'."

Rand shot him a perplexed look.

"What the hell?"

Winston chuckled.

"See you later, son."

Then it was just the three of them.

"I'm going to let you two get acquainted," Spota said and walked back to his punching bag in the corner. Rhodes gave a faint nod.

"Okay, Rand. I went through your file this morning," Rhodes said. "From what I can tell and what I've read, you don't have any background in martial arts. You've been in some street fights and played some sports, but you're more of a brawler, not a fighter."

Rand nodded.

"Here is the bottom line," Rhodes continued. "We want speed, agility and ability to adapt. Bulk? Huge muscles? Overrated. Trust me. You want to be able to strike quick. If you hit first, hit fast and hit in the right place, it doesn't matter how big you are or how much you can bench press, understand?" Then not waiting for an answer. "Remember speed. Strike first. Strike hard."

"Yes sir."

"Shit, cut the sir. I'm only about seven years older than you. I appreciate the respect, but you're part of a team now. Equals. Got it?"

"Got it."

"Good. How's your shoulder? How's that bullet wound coming along?"

"Only slightly tender. I can't believe how I recovered so fast. I can rotate it fine. It doesn't affect my grip or hand movement very much."

"And it's your right shoulder?"

Rand nodded.

"Damn. That will be a liability, but we'll work around it, understand?"

"Yes sir, I mean, of course. Sure."

"How's your leg?"

"Great. I can't even tell I was shot."

"Good. Okay, first of all, when it comes to hand to hand combat, forget that shit you see in the movies. There is no ten minute, flipping, table throwing, glass shattering boxing matches. You usually get one punch so it has to count. So here's the deal. You get one hit, where you going to strike?"

"Well, I would usually go for the jaw, maybe the nose?"

"Not bad, not bad, but –"

"What about the chest? I've never really hit anyone in the chest. Would that knock the air out of them?"

"No, forget the chest. Everyone is built different. Some people might fall down, others would laugh at you. You get one hit. Don't dance. Don't plan on a combo. Don't do any of that. Try to balance yourself and put your full body into it and hit them in the throat. Right in the Adam's Apple."

"The throat?"

"Yep, everybody's weak spot. You can't work out enough to protect it. You can't fake with it. You can't switch or feign. Hit them in the Adam's apple as hard as you can. If you miss, maybe you get their nose. The nose isn't bad either, it shocks them a bit and can make their eyes water, but, trust me on this Rand. You get one hit. Hit them in the throat. These guys don't play. They don't wrestle, they don't dance, they don't talk shit before a fight. Their job is to either subdue or kill. Period. You have to shut them down immediately. Kill or be killed. If the throat doesn't work, you hit them in the balls."

"The balls? Really? I thought a gentleman never did that."

"Who said anything about being a gentleman?" A smile flashed across the face for an instant, then disappeared. "Kill or be killed. You of all people should know that by now."

"Yeah, I guess so…I just thought things might be different."

"Different? Shit. Different, where? Out here? Shit. What you saw and did in Austria is the real deal from what I read. What you went through is par for the course. There are no more rules, except the ones you make. Got it?"

"Got it."

"Now, let me see what you've got."

Rhodes handed Rand a pair of boxing gloves. Rand had never worn anything like them, felt the thick, cushioned padding unnatural. Could not wriggle his fingers. They felt like dead weights on the end of his arm. Rhodes picked up two boxing punch mitts, stuffed his long hands into them. Lifted his arms up. Positioned one on each side of his body.

"Okay, let me just get a look to see what I can work with. Just throw some punches and try to hit the mitts. One up, one down. Stay focused."

Rand stepped back, aimed his shoulder, threw his best punch at the glove, a wide right Irish hook as he called it. It had never let him down in a fight. His one good move, he always said.

The punch landed solidly on the mitt. Rhodes didn't budge. Didn't flinch.

"Okay. Decent power. But that wide arc hook isn't going to cut it. This ain't Jack Dempsey. This ain't Rocky or Cinderella Man. Remember, you need short, quick, fast jabs."

"Jabs to the throat."

"That's right. Jabs to the throat"

"One shot. That's it. Kill or be killed."

"Kill or be killed."

Rhodes gave a silent nod. The sparkle gone from his eyes. The dark globes stared back at him. Level. On guard.

CHAPTER FIFTY-TWO

R and was sipping on a concoction that Spota had brought them, "Guaranteed to re-hydrate you and then some." It tasted faintly fruity. Rand could taste traces of coconut water, and was that pineapple or ginger? But the rest of the liquid was a mystery. He had sweated out the wine from the previous night and, despite the soreness in his upper body from working on his jabs all morning, felt a shot of energy course through his veins.

"So, what exactly is in this?" He asked Spota. "Like super Gatorade or something?"

"Something like that. I don't really know, but it works," Spota said. "Hell, I drink it whether I've been working out or not. It's good for you and I need all the hydration I can get in this heat."

"Do they put steroids or anything like that in this? Vitamin B? Adrenaline boosts?" Rand asked.

Rhodes laughed. "Not that we know of. They say it is all natural and I haven't gotten any taller or stronger, but there sure is something in it, that gives a little eye-opener. Speaking of eye-opener," Rhodes said, "Let me teach you one more skill before you go off with demolition man, here."

Back to the middle of the room. The gloves back on. Heavy thick clumsy things on his arms. Rand was having trouble, his arms starting to quiver and spasm under the underused duress.

"Okay, Rand. We talked offense, but here is your defense. When you are in a fight, any block will do. Yeah, if you can throw hammer fist or inside block or a parry. But the bottom line is even lifting your arms in front of your face will work."

"Really? Like a clinch? That just seems so…basic."

"It doesn't matter how it looks, you just want it to work."

"So no Judo or martial arts, leg sweeps?"

"We don't have time. I've got one, maybe, two days to teach you. So I can teach you 10 moves to execute poorly that you probably won't recall in the adrenaline of a fight, or two moves to execute precisely. My mantra is two perfect moves beat 30 okay moves any day. You played football right?"

"Yeah."

"Mainly defense, but some offense, right?"

"Yeah, linebacker and a little tight end."

"Then you'll understand. If you can execute two plays to near perfection or get lost in a playbook and try to use 30, which would you do?"

"I would say two, but during the course of a game, your opponent can figure out what you're doing and adjust to it."

"Well put. But here's the difference. You aren't fighting for a game, but for a minute. Understand?"

"Yes." Rand wiped the sweat trickling down his brow with the back of the glove. Blinked. And focused.

CHAPTER FIFTY-THREE

Three eggs, four sausage patties and two biscuits later, and Rand felt his eyelids drooping. His arms ached. His shoulder had flared up during his defense session with Rhodes. Had taken a quick shower and now was ready for a nap. Instead, he was sitting at one of the cafeteria tables, guzzling coffee. The cafeteria offered just about everything you could want for breakfast, Spota had told him. And the best part of it is with people working shifts, you can eat dinner for breakfast or breakfast for dinner.

"Well, hot damn," Rand had replied. "This is a regular Waffle House."

Spota laughed. "Yeah, I guess so, except the food is a ton better here and the chance of you running into any chaotic sloppy drunks is much less."

"Speaking of chaos," Rand said, lifting another cup of coffee to his eager lips, "how did you wind up here? Conscription? Use the old drunk sailor trick? What's your story?"

"How did I get here? Well, let's see. In a nutshell, I'd been kicked out of Special Ops. I studied for several years, but got bored with theoretical and wanted real action. Then I worked jobs in Bolivia, Ukraine, Japan, you name it. I worked for the small contractors or big countries, that, well, needed a favor, you know the highest bidder is the name of the game, I've also -"

"Don't let the bravado fool you," Winston's voice interrupted him as the man sat down beside Rand.

"Sir?" Rand said.

"Don't let all that bravado fool you. Spota here likes to talk like he's a grade one bad ass, a real action hero bad boy – and he is sometimes -" a nod toward Spota. "But, I bet he left out the part that before he joined the armed forces he completed his under-graduate degree in Chemistry and Geology in two years."

Spota hung his head and gave a self-deprecating shrug and chuckle.

Winston continued.

"Yeah, he probably also didn't tell you about the graduate work he did for kicks at Berkeley, Boulder or in Switzerland did he?"

Spota kept his head down, but Rand could see he was suppress-ing a grin.

"And, probably, he passed on the work he's done for us...am I right, Spota?"

Finally, the head lifted, the face tried to stifle a smile.

"No, sir. You know I didn't want to give him the whole story, just a briefing, sir."

"Shit," Winston spat. "No, you wanted to sound like Jason Statham's crazy ass cousin, but that's okay. You see here Rand. He deserves some room to brag. He's the best damn demolitions man around. Bonus? If he ever gets bored with us, he's smart enough to get on with any top university teaching, but I don't think he'd ever want to exchange this party to hang out with some stuffed shirts at a dandy school, would you?"

"No sir," Spota said. "I am quite content, here."

He shot Rand a wink.

"Good. Well, I hate to break up your get-to-know-me club, but Rand, Eliot wants to see you."

Rand slowly stood, already feeling the muscle strain he knew would double in the next 24 hours, old muscles being pushed into shape, new ones slow to develop.

"Ah, Winston," he said, stifling a yawn. "Can I bring my coffee?"

CHAPTER
FIFTY-FOUR

Winston had not even accompanied him to the shaded path that led to The Library.

"You know where it is and damned if I'm going further out in the sun if I can help it."

Rand lumbered toward The Library, still finding its otherworldly visage portentous as it sat alone at the end of the shaded path amidst the flatlands. He didn't bother knocking. Walked in. Back through the tunnel of bookshelves. The grand cone of light ahead. Eased through its shimmering magnificence, toward the corner where he assumed Eliot waited.

He stopped in front of the map on the wall. It still intrigued him. He felt pulled to it as he did the day before. Some odd lure of the lines and symbols. Was something familiar here, he wondered? Did something make sense? He moved closer to it. Squinted to read any of the small words. Wanted something to click for him. To make sense. A voice broke the spell.

"How are you today, Rand?" Eliot asked. Rand gazed into the darkness, could see the outline of the man sitting in the same chair as the day before.

"Fine. A little bit sore from my work out this morning, but fine, I guess."

"Good. I know we weren't able to finish our conversations yesterday and I wanted to talk with you some more one-on-

one, to see if I could help you understand us anymore before the others join us for a meeting later for our mission, or, shall we call it a quest?"

Rand offered a wry smile.

"Yes sir. A quest."

"I see the map has caught your eye again."

"Yes sir. What is it exactly? I recognize some of these symbols. I don't know what they mean, but I've seen them before on the map my grandfather left me and on the standing stones back in Austria."

"Yes, I believe you have. Those symbols are Atlantean and that map, Rand, is Atlantis."

"Atlantis?"

"Yes."

"Atlantis. Damn. Kent said it was true, showed me some standing stones with these same symbols on them, but still…A map of it? This is unreal."

A smile from Eliot. A glimmer in the eyes.

"Yes. Yes it is. It was a glorious civilization. Something we could talk about for years on another day. The standing stones you saw in The Castle were some of the last relics. We do not have any. I saw them several times, oh, the last time was, dear me, decades ago." A far off look in his eyes.

"Okay, but where was it? Atlantis. Is it completely destroyed like Kent said or were they hiding it somewhere, somehow?"

"No, no, my child. It is gone. Forever, I'm afraid. No one ever found it, because they looked for it in all the wrong places. Our greatest deception of all outside of the lost knowledge of Slendoc Meridian, is Atlantis. The fact is, it was never in the Atlantic Ocean. It was located about 180 miles south of what is now Fiji."

"That is completely fu-, I mean screwed up," Rand said. "You've got to be kidding me. I mean, the mythology, the writings of Plato - or was it Aristotle? – even the name itself for The Atlantic Ocean. Are you serious?"

"Yes, yes I am. We filtered and grew all those deceptions, great deceptions through the centuries to keep the original place hidden. Its original name was not even Atlantis, but rather Son Pacificus."

"And you said it is located in the Pacific?"

"Yes, it is. Or was. Our last attempt to salvage what we could was in 1974. Unfortunately, we experienced rather significant losses when an unfortunate event triggered an earthquake and, subsequently, a tsunami. We lost all our crew. When we returned a year later, everything we had initially found was lost. Buried. Destroyed. Completely. Irrevocably."

"I find it hard to believe," then realizing how much of this strange new world he had stumbled into since that afternoon in early June when the lawyer from Haskins & Hall delivered him the letter from his grandfather, everything had become believable.

"It is hard to believe," Eliot said. "Which is why we judged our deception of it, successful. But, think about it, Rand. Have you ever looked at a map of the Pacific? Great gaping ocean. Wide seas with nothing for miles upon miles, but the random atoll. That's where it was. A sizable subcontinent, located around Fiji, north of New Zealand, part of the vast Pacific Rim as they call it. It was lost to the ages, but, thankfully before its final destruction we retrieved what we needed to before it was lost forever."

"And, let me guess what that was?" Rand said. "Pieces of The Slendoc Meridian."

"Yes, yes," Eliot said. "A few last slivers. It was The Slendoc Meridian that helped that country rise to the pinnacle of civilizations and then what led them to their utmost destruction as well. We use it or it uses us. We are weak. There is no in between, no compromise. Now it is time for the destruction of it and for our species to make it on our own."

"Eliot," Rand said. "I have another question that has been nagging at me."

"Yes. Please ask all. I will answer everything I can."

"When I was back there, in Austria, Hope talked about some type of master plan Kent had. Some type of completion of a cycle with that piece of the stone I, well, they found from my grandfather's map. What was that? What type of master plan?"

"Kent thought with that last bit of power that they could find a way to finally build his master race of humanity. That with the power of the stone they could develop the technology to wean out the weaker of us –"

"Weaker of us? What do you mean?"

"Us. Our species. The weaker. He meant the disabled. The mentally ill. The poor. Many non-white races. Most of Africa. A large part of Asia and South America. All those who he considered inferior. From what I gather, he was going to use the stones to induce a way to eradicate an entire group of people off the globe –"

"What," Rand gave a bitter laugh. "Like some super weapon?"

"No, no. As with many things, he was going to use the power, the influence of the stones to aid in creating a way to do this in a subtle manner. Hyper-creation with a group of select scientists. He wanted to create something like a disease that only affected certain groups of people. Or by genetic selection via viruses, but not only viruses toward people, but also toward environments. Drought. Pestilence. Drugs introduced to certain segments of society, like the potato blight in Ireland and crack in urban America in the 1980s. We think he was working on a biological warfare. Something to that effect. I am not exactly sure of his method, but we know his intention. A final plan. His master plan, you might say."

"A master plan? What to create a master race? That is preposterous. That sounds like what the Nazis tried."

Eliot stared at him hard. The friendly crinkle gone from around the eyes. The eyes focused. Any glint of light. Extinguished.

"And that, my child," he said, "was when we split the first time last century."

CHAPTER
FIFTY-FIVE

The scrape of wood on marble from the front of the building echoed roughly toward them.

"Ah, that would be the door," Eliot said. "They are a bit early, but that will do."

"Who's they?"

"The team. Our team. For the mission. The quest as you like to call it. Now is the time to talk of the slaying of dragons, my child," he motioned with his hand toward a dim corner behind him. "There is a round card table back there. Would you be kind enough to set it up for us? We have much to discuss and Tempus Fugit."

CHAPTER
FIFTY-SIX

It might have been a round table, but there was no pomp and circumstance about it. No chalices or candles or glimmering steel swords set in a symmetrical circus. Instead, several large maps and cups of tea in front of six chairs for Eliot, Mary Celest, Rhodes, Spota, Winston and Rand.

"Well, let's get started," Eliot said once they all arrived, a green eyeshade visor perched on his head to shield against the light. "You all know each other and we – with the exception of Rand –reviewed this plan several times. Of course, Winston's addition has added some new wrinkles, but I believe we are in firm shape. However, with us less than 24 hours out, I want to fill in Rand, review any changes and see if everything is in place. Questions?"

Winston? What? Wasn't he retired? Rand shot him a questioning look.

"That's right son," Winston said as if reading his thoughts. "This cowboy's gonna saddle up for one more ride. See what the noise is about and raise a little hell."

"He also," interjected Eliot, "adds some serious experience and gravitas to our crew. No offense to you younger chaps, but Winston will be playing the role of a supervisor and with his demeanor and experience, looks the part."

"Playing the role?" Rand asked.

"Ah, let me explain," Eliot said. "Winston will be assuming the role of a supervisor for an engineering firm that specializes in foundation repair."

He let the words sit.

"Excuse me," Rand said, "but with all due respect, what the hell is going on?"

A thin smile from Eliot, though Rand thought he detected a passing flash of merriment in his eyes.

"Here's the picture Rand. The Organization's North American headquarters is located in the Gila National Forest, about eight hours west, southwest from here at a place called Black Sands. Black Sands is a cover for what they claim is bio-engineering and biological experimentation, though we have heard other stories that they also experiment on...other living things," then gathering himself, "From our intelligence gathering, we discovered the stones are housed in the main building in the third floor beneath the surface. The wall on the north side of the building is weak in several places. This is a combination of faulty construction and natural shifts of the sediment layers in that region. Earlier today, we detonated a small bomb several miles away on a specific fault line which triggered a minor earthquake. According to our expert," and here, he nodded at Spota, "the quake itself was minor, but with the device in the right place will be just enough to cause minor structural damage."

"That's right, sir," said Spota. "Nothing too crazy, but I've been studying this area for several months and found some fault lines we used to help this process along. I've calculated and re-calculated everything hundreds of times and what we did today should be just enough to cause some structural damage. Maybe something serious, maybe not, but definitely some cracks that should get them worried. Worried enough to call in experts. And the experts will be us."

The levitious smile.

"Wait, wait, wait," Rand said, the words spluttering out of his mouth faster than he intended, "We're going eight hours from here. Eight hours? We are that close to these guys?"

"You got it," Winston said. "What did I tell you when we got here? Hide in plain sight."

"Then," Rand continued, bordering on incredulous. "You said we're going in as experts?"

Eliot slowly raised his hand. His eyes closed.

"Rand, Rand. Hear the plan out. It may sound mad as a March hare, but, trust us, we've thought this out. And the 'we' that Spota referred to," here he opened his eyes, "was not all of us, but, rather him, you, Winston and Rhodes. Though at one time I was a rather dashing field operative, I will be here with Mary Celest. You all get to have the fun."

No one said anything for a moment. Rand looked around the table. All eyes on me, he thought.

"All right, I'll settle down for a minute and listen. Sorry, this just sounds, uh, I don't know..." he grabbed his cup of tea, took a long, deliberate swallow.

"Sounds crazy as a hog flying sideways is what it sounds like, son," Winston said. "But it's a good plan or I wouldn't be involved. Go ahead, Spota. Finish up."

Spota took a deep breath, looked around the table, then at Rand.

"Okay, like I said, we triggered a minor earthquake. When Black Sands does have infrastructure work done it is outsourced to a specific company in Albuquerque, but, let's just say they all have food poisoning right now. Since we triggered the earthquake, we've been monitoring the phone lines for every foundation repair and construction company within 150 miles. We intercepted their call for help this morning and now are sending in a team dressed as construction workers to repair the structure. We leave tomorrow morning. First thing. We've been faxed over the confidentiality agreement and they have provided us with very strict orders on what we can and cannot bring. We will be scanned at the entrance so no weapons, cell phones, recording devices, anything. Our job is to infiltrate. Set charges and get out, right? These charges are extremely powerful. They should react with the stones and cause terrific destruction. But, due to the volatility of the charges, it will have a massive impact and possible aftershocks, we –"

"And Rand," Eliot again. "This is where you come in. As I

mentioned, you are the only one among us who can withstand the pure power of the stones. You will go in with the crew, but then will go solo directly to the lowest level, remove the protective glass that houses the largest of these stones and place the explosives directly next to it. The other explosives you can leave throughout the room near the stones. The rest of the crew will install some faux hydraulics that have been filled with highly combustible explosives. Once your prime explosive detonates, it will have a massive ripple effect - a chain reaction - not only with the other stones, but with the other explosives we are bringing with us."

"Why don't we just bomb the place? With a plane or a launcher, or, whatever. I mean that would be a lot easier, right?"

Eliot nodded.

"Yes, it would. If it was only that easy. A bomb dropped on top might trigger a reaction, but it might just bury the stones further. To complicate it further, we can't just drop a bomb on it, because their airspace is restricted up to ten miles out as part of some quasi-research bill that they got the government to approve. That left us with one choice for success. Go in. Set the explosives directly beside the stones and then detonate."

Winston interrupted.

"In other words. You set them. You get out. That is it. We don't have time for delving into research or liberating files or anything else. This isn't a tour. We need to do the task and leave. This is a one shot situation. Period."

Rand noticed all eyes were on him. Realized the point of the entire meeting was him. Was he being evaluated? Tested? Were they looking for a reaction?

"Okay," Rand said, feeling the odd urge to raise his hand. "This is good and well enough, but how are we supposed to get these explosives in? Bribe the guards? Assemble them on the inside? Pray we don't get caught?"

Spota shifted in his chair. Looked at everyone around the table. Cracked a grin.

"I could tell you, but I'd rather show you."

CHAPTER
FIFTY-SEVEN

A half an hour later and Rand was still soaking it in. His years in the newsroom and instincts gave him the innate ability to wean the difference between someone who embellishes and someone with confidence. He had thought Spota was of the latter ilk and found his hunch had steered him true. However, the curve of the situation was, the man had only exaggerated his mischievousness, not his talent. As Winston had said, Spota completely downplayed his talent. A fact that Rand was rapidly discovering.

"Okay, so here is the deal, my friend," Spota said. The two were sitting at a desk in Spota's 'Lab,' nothing more than an oversized conference room with an elongated table and two laptops. "Your average demolition man, saboteur, engineer whatever you call him, just knows how to blow stuff up. How to destroy it. And that usually involves a little bit of creativity, but mainly, a lot of explosives - Gelignite, C4, all that good stuff. But, the key to massive, succinct, almost guaranteed success of annihilation is not just quantity of explosives, but the quality of the workmanship in demolition. You can study the situation, finding weaknesses, exploiting them and creating advantages within your environment to aid the process, got it?"

Rand hesitated. "I think so...like, using a certain type of explosive, gas, uh, I don't know that will burn stronger with certain materials, or types of gas that burn hotter in certain climates, maybe in certain altitudes?"

Spota slapped the table.

"Close, real close. Materials and geology."

"Okay."

"First, materials. Like I said, a lot of people just use more – Gelignite, C4 and dynamite are good, but can be unstable. Have you heard of HMX?"

"No."

"Let's see, how about Semtex? Plastic explosives?"

"Yes. Easy to transport, fairly cheap. IRA stuff, right? Is that what you're talking about?"

"Got it. So, anyway, HMX is military grade plastic explosives to simplify it. Super hard to get. But we got it. What we did for this job was package it in the most non-threatening things you can imagine. Hammers, screwdrivers and, most importantly, egg timers."

"Tools? Egg timers? You got to be kidding me."

"Yeah, we're going into this place, they're going to be monitoring the hell out of us. We can't just walk in there with a bunch of damn explosives so we camouflage that shit, compress the hell out of it and hide it in plain sight. Plus check this out. We've got a special spray that bonds with the exterior so if they run our toolboxes through an X-Ray machine, you see exactly what you want - a hammer or a screwdriver. The egg timers are the best because we have an automatic clock already installed to set off the explosives without any extra packaging."

"How does this all work, though? Some type of reflection or built it image it projects to the X-Ray?"

"Hell, if I know. I just make the explosives and leave it to the boys upstairs for the smoke and mirrors."

CHAPTER
FIFTY-EIGHT

"So is this the new look for fall? Is this what all the cool kids will be wearing?" Rand asked.

Spota laughed. Rhodes didn't. Winston shook his head. They were back in the gym. The four of them. Spread out on the floor were four outfits that matched the cliché of what every construction worker might wear.

Dusty gray work shirt, a zipper in front. A patch on the right chest said, 'Foundation Worx.' Blue jeans. Brown work boots, the color of dead leaves. And a hard hat, with a clear visor that could be swiveled up or down.

"These are our uniforms," Winston said. "They are ugly, but have quite a few tricks as the boys upstairs made some modifications."

"What kind of modifications?" Rand asked.

"You ever hear of Dragon Skin?"

"You mean the heavy metal band that did a cover of a Monkees' song?"

Winston blew out his breath. "Son, you better be glad you're funny or I would be tempted to just whup your ass half the time you speak."

"Sorry, Winston. You just kind of tossed me a soft ball there. I mean Dragon Skin? Really?"

Winston smiled. Continued.

"Anyway, Dragon Skin is a bullet proof material in case we run into any trouble. It is not as rigid as Kevlar. It uses more interlocking plates, allows better motion and is lighter, got it?"

"Yes, sir."

"So, we took the basic premise, but have developed it into not only body armor, but armor in the guise of a shirt, pants, hard hat and a visor. I even have some gloves for you which are not only bullet proof, but also deliver a hell of a wallop without hurting you in case you have to throw a punch."

"So, you mean, I can wear this stuff and get shot and be okay?"

"Not exactly okay," Winston said. "You'll have a bruise, but, yeah, unless you get hit by a 50 caliber machine gun a dozen times at close range, you should be fine. Actually we got some time before we leave. Hey, Rhodes, how about giving him a demonstration?"

CHAPTER
FIFTY-NINE

"How does the shirt feel?" Rhodes asked.

"It's fine, I mean, It isn't exactly fine Egyptian cotton, but for stopping bullets, I can put up with a little scratchiness."

Rhodes almost smiled.

"Good. Now I am going to shoot you."

"What?"

"Chill out. There is a chance you will be shot when we go in there. You can be in shock when it happens or be prepared, or, accustomed to the blow."

"But, won't that bruise me? Knock the breath out of me?"

"Yeah, if I was shooting an average bullet, it would probably knock you back a bit, maybe if it hit you in the chest knock the breath out of you. But, I'm going to use a rubber bullet and trust me, you need to be ready to be shot. Otherwise, you'll freeze up. If you get in this situation you won't have time for stopping and thinking. Like I keep telling you, you need to be ready to act. To react. And fast. Got it?"

Misdirection. Misinformation. Then fast action. Rand remembered his grandfather's mantra.

"Yes."

"Okay, go to the end of the room."

Rand walked slowly, double checking to make sure the zipper was tight, pulling his sleeves down on his wrist trying to make them overlap the gloves. Any extra layer of protection.

"Okay, that's far enough. Now turn around and run at me. Run at me and hit me. Disable me."

"What?"

"You heard me. Do it."

Rand started walking towards Rhodes.

"I said run, bitch!"

Rhodes raised the gun, leveled it and fired. The bullet hit Rand in the bicep, threw his shoulder back. Rand stumbled. Felt a sting in his shoulder. Stared at Rhodes.

"I said run! What are you waiting for!" The gun raised again. Another shot echoed in the room. This one struck Rand in the stomach, just under his left ribcage. He stumbled back again. Tried not to double over.

"Damn!" Rand yelled. "What the hell?"

"Run!"

Rhodes went to squeeze the trigger. Rand ran toward him. The sound of a gunshot. Rand felt the bullet hit his shin. Almost stumbled, but half-hopped on one leg, not slowing now. Anger pushing him against the pain. Rhodes fired again. Rand felt nothing. Had Rhodes missed? It didn't matter. He was closing in. 15 feet. 10 feet. He winced, but kept running. 5 feet. Then, lunging at Rhodes, arm cocked the way he had learned. A quick jab. To the throat. He punched. Put all of his force into that one move. Saw his fist moving to the Adam's apple. Then an arm knocked it out of the way. A block. Felt a force at the back of his calves. His legs swept from under him. Then he was on the mat. Eyes staring at the ceiling. Damn. He had failed. He saw Rhodes face over him. A smile. A hand reached down. Rand grabbed it and Rhodes helped him up.

Rand was breathing hard. Tiny sparks before his eyes. His head swimming, the tinges of a headache forming. He leaned over to put his hands on his knees

"Whoa, whoa," Rhodes grabbed his hands, stopped him.

"What?"

"No. No rest. Never let them see you tired, rule one. It will confuse them. Rule two. Never let yourself envision yourself as tired.

Stay straight. No time for rest. No time for recovery."

"That's," ragged breaths. "That's bullshit. You just shot me, then did some damn karate stuff and swept my legs? I need to rest."

"Nope. Never. Stand up. When you're in a situation, you have no time for rest. For recovery. You have to train yourself."

"Doesn't matter. I failed anyway."

"Failed?"

"Yeah, that was a joke." Rand felt shame. Like the first time he tried out for football. Was lost. No skill. Just powered through it fueled by anger. Knew he was sloppy. Unaware.

"Hell," Rhodes said. "That wasn't half-bad. You came on strong after the first two shots. Not bad at all. What did you think?"

"That was terrible. And painful. Damn. I can't believe you really shot me."

"And yet," Rhodes said. "And yet, you know I am glad I did. You were shocked. And now you know what it will feel like. Preparation is nothing without experience."

CHAPTER SIXTY

Two bland, white work vans whistled along south I-25, gliding at a steady 70 miles per hour. They were bullet-proof and had enhanced engines, but appeared completely innocuous. 'Foundation Worx' was stenciled in tan on their sides, along with a phone number and website.

Winston and Rhodes rode in the front van, Spota and Rand followed behind them, Spota driving, Rand quiet, staring out the window. They had left after breakfast. Rand had slept fitfully the night before. The team had somberly dined on slabs of bison, mixed greens and baked potatoes before each going their own way. Entering his room, Rand found a copy of 'Dubliners' by James Joyce by his bed. He showered and slipped beneath the cool covers, his body begging for rest. But, despite the weariness in his body, his mind would not surrender to sleep and he read the entire book before drowsiness overtook him shortly after midnight.

Now, it was nearing noon, the monotonous highway stared back at him and he emptied the contents of a small cooler he had been given.

"Okay, Spota, we've got turkey on rye, turkey on wheat, granola bars, bananas, apples and water. What do you want?"

"It doesn't matter to me. You pick first."

"This isn't much of a last meal, is it? I mean, if we're going to die, we should be at a steakhouse somewhere," Rand said, passing a sandwich and a bottled water to Spota.

"Thanks, but no thanks on the water."

"No water?"

"Hey, water is good for you, but I've got some of that special drink we had during your workout. Like I said, I drink it all the time. I'm also on good terms with the dietitian and she gave me a couple of extra shots of B-12 in this batch. You want some?"

"Sure. Why not?"

"That's right. Smart man. It's behind my seat. Pull it up and take a chug. You can't beat this stuff. Energy and focus, without getting jittery."

"You sound like a commercial. Are you going to market this after we're done?"

Spota laughed. "Oh, that would be great wouldn't it? Sit on TV all day, talking shit about how some drink is a miracle elixir, surrounded by a couple of fine ladies, getting paid the big bucks."

"Seriously though," Rand asked. "What you are going to do after this? If, well, if we succeed."

"Okay, I've got it planned out. We do this job. Hit the safe house. Lay low for a week or two. Then, bam, the beach. And, not just any beach. I am going to the Baja California Sur. A super small town on the beach in western Mexico. Blue Pacific Ocean. Lots of rays. Very few tourists. Cold drinks with umbrellas in them and some fine ladies serving them, preferably in bikinis."

"Bikinis on your mind?"

Spota laughed. "Hey, I guess so. It's been a while, I'll leave it at that. But, what about you? What are you going to do? Going back to hang out with Eliot and Mary Celest? Striking out on your own?"

Rand stared out the window, the blur of beige and burnt green.

"My friend, I honestly haven't even thought about it."

"Well, you better think about it now, my man."

"Yeah, I guess so."

"I mean, once we get the green light to leave the safe house, you can do whatever you want, right? They always give us lots of cash, I.D.s and then a number to call if we want to come back in. Most of us disappear. I see some now and again, like Rhodes, but you're different. No offense, but we both know it, right?"

Rand issued a mirthless laugh.

"Yeah, I sure am…I don't know what I'll do. Relaxing on a beach does sound like a tonic for a tired soul, I will say that. At the same time, I feel like I need to go back. I mean, I want to go back. I, this might sound cheesy, but I need to know more about my family, about what they did or wanted to do…I want to know more and I don't know where else I will get any answers…I don't know."

"Sounds fine to me. Family is important. Whether you're running to them or from them, they are a part of life. But, if you change your mind, the offer is open for you to come with me to the beach. I usually like to travel solo, but you're pretty laid back. Also, we would make a good team with the ladies."

Rand laughed again.

"You sure are about the ladies today. Goodness."

"Hey, it beats thinking about what we're getting ready to do."

CHAPTER SIXTY-ONE

"How y'all doin' back there?" Winston's voice coughed through the static on Spota's radio.

"Good, chief, we're good."

"How's our wonder boy? Rand, can you hear me?"

Spota handed the walkie-talkie over to Rand.

"Yes, sir."

"Son, you're gonna do fine. I want you and Spota to go over the plan again and then brief you on what we do after we pull this off, okay?"

"Yes, sir."

"Good. Good. We're about an hour out, so we'll be cutting contact after this call, okay? Everybody relax, this is going to be as easy as pie. You good, Rand?"

"Yes, sir."

"You got any questions for me?"

A hundred smart ass comments flet through Rand's mind, though none of them seemed appropriate.

"No, sir."

"Good, hand me back over to Spota then."

"Yes, sir." Rand passed the walkie-talkie back, tried to hide a faint shaking of nervousness in his hand.

"Spota, have you reviewed everything and gone over the escape plan with him?"

"Not exactly."

"Like I just told Rand, this would be a good time for it."

"Yes, sir."

"All right, we're going into the mountains so hang loose. Over and out then. See you in a few."

CHAPTER SIXTY-TWO

"**A**ll right, Rand. Here is the deal. We do what we have to do. Should only be there an hour tops. Just enough to install these hydraulics, let me and Winston dazzle them with our knowledge of engineering, give them a lot of paperwork to sign. We promise to come back tomorrow with a full crew and that shit. You'll walk around, do what you need to do. Go into that special room and set the alarm on the egg timers so they explode at 4:15 p.m. Got it? After you set everything, meet us back at the vans at 4 p.m. We'll be waiting for you and ready to go. If we can get 15 minutes away from Black Sands, we should be okay when the fireworks start."

"That is a tight turnaround."

"Yeah," then reaching into his pocket. "Meant to give you this earlier."

He handed Rand a Mickey Mouse wind-up watch.

"Well," Rand said. "I really don't know what to say. I mean, really, I have no idea what to say. Why are you giving me a Mickey Mouse watch?"

"We need to be out of there at 4 p.m., got it?"

"Yes."

"And from what Winston told me, the stones can fry any electronic or electric equipment right?"

"Yes."

"So, here you go. Wind-up. Analog. Old school. This is synchronized to all our watches so we should all be on the same page."

"What if this messes up, I mean, if it reacts."

"Well, then you get to improvise."

Shit, Rand thought. No pressure.

"Any questions?" Spota asked.

"I don't know. You guys aren't giving me a lot of time to mull this over. And there is a lot of 'possible improvisation.' I mean, y'all have a lot of confidence in me, especially considering I didn't even know you a week ago."

"Ha," a half laugh. "I don't know about y'all, but Eliot does and that is good enough for us and for what it is worth, I think you'll do fine. I have a good instinct on these things."

"Okay," Rand exhaled.

"All right, now here is the escape plan. We take these vans in, but when we leave, we'll abandon the vans and all pile into a Humvee we've got waiting and head south towards the Mexican border."

"So, where is this Humvee?"

"Just about four miles from the site. We dropped it during the earthquake mayhem. When that happened, they had some short circuiting with the monitors and satellite feeds for few minutes, so we just drove it off the highway onto an old logging road, parked it and left it."

"So you've got a Humvee just, sitting out in the woods?"

"Yeah, more or less. But check this out. It's covered in a Vatec-type camouflage wrap – basically an invisibility cloak, a piece of cloth that bends light and reflections to blend into the background. It is pretty much impossible to pick up by satellite unless they are using infrared scanning and the engine is running."

"So, you, we, just left it there?"

"Yeah."

"What if, I don't know, someone stumbles across it?"

"Not much we can do. It's not like anyone can break into it. If a random sweep finds it somehow? Oh well, it's a risk we got to take."

"Hell of a risk."

"Again, that's why I am thinking of the girls in bikinis."

Rand was silent for a moment. Then, "But, wait a second, aren't we going to look a little conspicuous driving around New Mexico and, especially, Mexico in a Humvee?"

Spota laughed.

"This is no showroom canary yellow Humvee you see driving around in Atlanta. We've got a specialized one. Basically, it is a specialized M1151 model with a ton of modifications like raised suspension so we can clear most boulders and not get stuck anywhere. It also has stronger armor – not that we should need it, but do you know what my favorite part is?"

"What's that?"

"It can go over 150 miles per hour. That may not sound impressive to you, Rand, but your average Humvee only hits about 70."

"Okay."

"And we won't be driving it around Mexico. We just take it to the safe house and leave it there. We mainly need it in case we have to go off road for any reason."

A dozen reasons for going off road sped through Rand's mind, but he pushed them back.

"Plus," Spota continued. "It also has a ton of other gadgets such as predictive and evasive operating systems in case we come up on a gulch we can't see. And it's filled with all kinds of goodies if we need them. Guns, gadgets, grenades. It's a beautiful piece of machinery."

"I've never thought of machinery as beautiful."

"Ha, that's because you've never seen me drive."

CHAPTER
SIXTY-THREE

Rugged cliff walls hugged the road as the vans wove through the ocher mountains. The mid-afternoon sun came and went, sometimes hidden behind the hills, sometimes half-eclipsed behind a thicket of Ponderosa Pines.

"Almost there, almost there," Spota said.

"Good," Rand said. "It's been a long ride. Too much time to think about everything. Let's get this over with."

"I agree, my friend."

They crested over the backbone of a ridge and began their descent into a snug valley of black sand. Dark, rich, and yet, almost porous, as if it was used coffee grounds and you could sink into it, Rand thought. And yet, the valley sparkled. Geodesic biodomes scattered like marbles in an absurd geometry tossed across the basin's floor. In the middle of the valley was the main building. It was not iridescent, but bland, almost brutalist in its architecture. Massive thick legs of yellowed concrete encased a small band of blue windows that ribboned the exterior. An ugly iron door. It reminded Rand of pictures of Soviet era government buildings or cheap college campuses built in the 1970s. No pillars or décor out front. Just a walkway of black asphalt faintly visible above the dark sands.

Surrounding the valley was a steel fence. At least 16 feet high. Laced with barbed wire at the top, its razor edges glittering in the sun. The vans eased to a stop at the entrance where a mechanical arm more akin to innocent parking garages than military facilities stood sentry, a small building beside it. Bland. White. Flat roof. Yet, with plenty of windows. Tinted.

A woman with frazzled blond hair wearing olive green military fatigues walked out and gave a wave complemented with an awkward smile. Rand saw Winston's window roll down. She walked over. He handed her a slip of paper with a generous grin. They began talking. Rand could not hear what they said, but saw her laugh and brush the hair back over her shoulder.

"Son of a bitch," Spota said. "Look at the sly old dog. Laying that Texas charm on thick."

"I believe it. And I don't believe it," Rand said.

Rand watched as she gathered herself, before motioning to the building. Four men exited. Clad in the same olive-colored clothing. Two way radios on their belt and, yes, as Rand guessed, Berettas strapped snug to their waists. Three of them wore basic military caps, but the man in charge had a black beret snug on his head. A clipboard held to his side.

He approached Winston's window. Lifted the clipboard. Looked at Winston. The two began talking. Winston stepped out. Rhodes did the same.

The man with the beret motioned to his men and the security ritual began.

Winston and Rhodes were patted down and metallic wands waved over their bodies. Rand could see Winston say something to the man in charge, a grin on his face. One of the guards laughed, nodded his head.

Winston motioned to Rand's van.

"Time to get our frisk on," Spota said.

He must have read the apprehension on Rand's face.

"Hey, easy money, man. Just relax," Spota said and gave him a wink. They opened their doors. A hot blanket of air pushing through the streams of air conditioning.

Back into the desert sun. A bead of sweat trickled down the side of his temple. The man in charge approached.

"Good afternoon."

"Afternoon," Rand said, trying to affect a tone between respect and boredom.

"Driver's license?"

"Yes sir," Rand fished in his pocket, handed it over.

"Let's see," the man thumbed through the sheaf of papers on his clipboard that rattled in the desert breeze. Stopped. Eyed Rand. Then the license. "So, you are David Peterson, correct?"

"Yes. Yes, sir. But you can call me Dave."

No expression on the face.

"Okay, Mr. Peterson. Where were you born?"

"Forest City, North Carolina."

"Good. And how old are you?"

"29, sir."

"Thank you. As I told your boss, sorry for the inconvenience, but this is our security protocol."

"No problem."

The man in charge gave a low whistle. Marginally tilted his head. Walked back to Winston while two guards took his place. Wordless, one began to pat down Rand, the other waving a wand over his body. Rand looked over to Spota who was going through the same experience. Winston, already finished, had plucked a cigarette from his pack and lit it, jawing with the man in charge in low tones. Rhodes looked bored. Sunglasses tight on his face. Arms crossed. A yawn.

The man in charge broke off his conversation with Winston and in a voice born from years of authority announced to the group.

"Good. Thanks gentlemen. We need to look inside the vans now."

"Have at it," Winston said. "Let me know if you find any change back there. I need all the money I can get working here."

A pair of guards, each armed with what looked like a small metal detector, entered Winston's van. Five minutes later they emerged. Satisfied, they moved to Rand's van.

CHAPTER
SIXTY-FOUR

Were they taking longer searching the second van, Rand wondered? Or was he paranoid? His watch tight on his wrist beckoned, but he didn't want to look at it. Stay calm, he told himself. Stay calm. Spota had assured him the tools were impervious to X-ray or anything else. The explosives packed tight and secretive in the handles of the tools. The egg timers impenetrable.

One guard emerged from the back.

"Okay, looks like everything checks out, we -"

"Hey, what the hell is this?" A shout as another guard pulled a toolbox out and held it away from him.

"It's a toolbox," Winston said matter of factly.

"No, in it. There's four egg timers in here."

Shit, thought Rand. What is Winston going to tell them, we're here to make egg fucking salad, he thought.

"Damn right, they're egg timers," Winston said. "Y'all won't let me bring my cell phone in, so how the hell else I am supposed to gauge when the hydraulics are set or when the arc welder is hot enough? You want me to guess? Trust my watch from Wal-Mart? Maybe you have a sundial on you I can borrow."

Rand laughed out loud. He didn't mean to. Just a release of nervous laughter. Then everyone laughed, except the guard who found them, whose face burnished red.

"He's right, he's right," the man in charge said, then to Winston.

"Sorry about that. These young guns get a little excited with nothing to do out here."

"Hell, I hear ya," Winston said. "If we didn't have a whorehouse near our place in Silver City, I think we'd all go stir crazy."

"All that's left is your cell phones," the man in charge said.

"Hand 'em over boys, no texting your girl friends or playing candy crush," Winston said. "Don't worry you'll get 'em on the way out."

Rand handed over the dummy cell phone he had received back at Lux. Registered in David Peterson's name from a fly-by-night cellular company near Phoenix.

"Also your walkie-talkies."

"Well, wait a second," Winston said. "If you insist that is fine, but these are short wave radios and we'll need to talk to each other since we'll be in different parts of the building. When you're dealing with foundation issues you don't want to be running back and forth comparing notes and sketches."

A silence. A serious crease on the man in charge's face.

"Makes sense. Keep the radios then. But you will be escorted throughout the site."

"Wouldn't expect anything less," Winston said.

CHAPTER
SIXTY-FIVE

They were directed to the rear of the main building where a yawning loading bay waited for them, its enormous mouth open, waiting like a steel maw where they unloaded their toolboxes, strapped tool belts around their waists and donned their hard hats. They were escorted through a scuff-marked hallway into the main part of the building which could be graciously called an atrium.

Under the sickly fluorescent lights and barren walls, Winston was talking to a short maintenance chief, whose concern clung to his mustached face.

"So, if my specs are correct," Winston said, a sheaf of papers in one hand. "The damage is here on the northern wall, right?"

"Yep. You got it. The north wall. Like I said on the phone, I don't think it's going to collapse right now, but my boss doesn't want me to take any chances."

"I understand," Winston said. "We've got two hydraulics back in the van, but I didn't want to bring them out until we knew what we were working with."

"No, please, bring them out. I don't want to take any chances. Even if it's just window dressing, let's put them up."

"Sounds like you've got a real hard ass for a boss."

"Yeah."

"I understand. Can you have your men wheel them out for me

while we take a look around?"

"Yes, sir."

"Good. Good. We're going to split up in teams. I understand you all want us in and out as fast as possible."

"Yes, sir. We just need a patch, a, uh, safety measures for today."

"I understand. How many levels in this building? Just a main floor?"

"No sir, we've got two floors below this one. But the big cracks are here."

"Yeah, that sounds typical," Winston said.

Rand continued to be impressed with the man's ability to act the part.

"What we'll do is my top man," he gestured toward Spota, "will help me up here where we will install the hydraulics. I'd like to send my other two guys down each level just to double check. We'll be back tomorrow with our high-tech crew so they can do an in-earth scan, but my goal today is just to analyze it and stabilize, okay?"

"Sounds fine with me. I'll just need to get them a guard each to escort them."

"A guard? Hell, I don't need a nanny, brother. They already cleared us at the gate. Come on, we're grown-ups." A dry laugh.

"Yes. Sorry, just protocol."

"Hell, it's always something," Winston paused. Looked at the ground. Eyes back up, a smile on his face. "Okay, I guess as much as you're paying us, it don't matter. Like I said, I just want to get done. There's a good ball game on tonight."

"Yes sir."

CHAPTER
SIXTY-SIX

The guard's name was 'Marshall,' according to his name tag. Rand didn't bother introducing himself and faked a yawn. "Whew, long day."

"Yeah," Marshall agreed.

"Well, let's get this over with."

The two were in an elevator descending to the bottom floor. The same dull steel reflections. Rand had watched the guard punch -3. Perfect, Rand thought. Just as their intelligence had told them. Everything was on schedule. The elevator stopped. Doors glided open and Rand was greeted by the sight of a long white corridor lit by a single curving LED light tube above that gave the off-white walls a ghostly glow. He stepped out, toolbox in one hand, a clipboard in the other and began walking ahead. Saw a lone figure toward the end of the hall. Two automatic sliding doors with a tint of dark blue behind the man. That was the room, Rand knew. His destination. Took a deep breath. Knew what he had to do. Knew it was coming soon.

"Okay, this shouldn't take long," Rand said.

He began walking, making sure his strides were not too fast. Measuring himself. Every 20 feet or so, they would come across a black door with a single knob. A white number etched on it. Rand eyed the doors, but knew it wasn't the entrance he was looking for. No sound from the guard behind him, but the squeaking of thick soled rubber boots off the linoleum floor.

Rand paused every few feet to peer at the ceiling, then down along a wall and at the floor. Occasionally, he would pull out a Post-It and stick it on a wall, scribble some nonsense on the clipboard and then resume walking.

"What are those for?" The guard asked.

"Just places that might need double checking later, following up. I don't see anything there now, but it would be worth keeping an eye on. Just being pro-active."

Rand lifted the cuff on his shirt. Checked his watch. 3:33. Damn. This was too tricky. Too much preciseness for an operation that relied on demolitions. Damn. Not enough time to prepare. Felt a trickle of sweat run down his temple. What did Shakespeare say? Better 3 hours too early, than a minute late? Something like that. Time to make a move, he told himself.

He sauntered down the hall. The figure ahead came into focus. The same outfit as the rest of the guards, but this one clutched an M-16. Rand purposefully didn't make eye contact, but targeted his eyes on the walls and ceiling. Walk slow. Deliberately, he told himself. Be self-absorbed. A scribble on the clipboard. The occasional muttering under his breath, using phrases like, "looks solid," or "good shape" or "strong." He uttered them almost like a mantra. He could feel the guard staring at him.

CHAPTER SIXTY-SEVEN

"**C**an I help you?" The accent was American, but bland with no inflection.

"Ah," Rand arched his eyebrows in feigned surprise. "I don't think so, we're making good time. I'm with Foundation Worx. We're fixing some structural damage up top and they wanted me to check this floor for any anomalies."

The guard grunted.

"Yeah, I heard you were coming after that weird earthquake the other day. And I thought we were in a moderate zone, but, that shows you how much our scientists really know. Anyway, how's it going?"

"Good, good. I've seen a few potential hazards along the corridor, but nothing that can't wait until we bring in more supplies tomorrow," then the words out of his mouth before he even knew it. "But, I do need to check in there," Rand motioned to the doors behind the guard. "I understand it is a rather large room with relatively few load bearing supports."

The guard shot Rand a serious look, then glancing over his shoulder: "Hey, Marshall, you know anything about this?"

Rand turned to see Marshall shrug.

"I don't know. I'm just escorting him around."

"Yeah, yeah. Okay. This room is off-limits. I'll need to get an override on this before you can pass."

"Here we go again, bureaucracy," Rand sighed forcefully.

"Yeah, red tape, but it is what it is and I'm not risking my neck on it."

CHAPTER
SIXTY-EIGHT

The guard lifted his collar to speak into a radio. Rand noted the earpiece that snaked from the man's collar. Could only hear one side of the conversation.

"Yeah, I need Ian, please."

A pause.

"Yes, sir. I've got one of the workers from the foundation company down here, and –"

Another pause.

"Yes, sir. He is. But, he said he needs to inspect the Blue Room. Something about load bearing walls, I –"

A pause.

"Yes, sir. Of course, I will have Marshall accompany him in. Yes sir. Of course, sir. I understand. Yes sir. Over and out."

Rand looked at the guard, raised his eyebrows.

"Well, are we set to go?"

"Yeah, the chief isn't happy about it, but go ahead. You've signed all the non-disclosure forms, so remember that. You've got five minutes max. Marshall, you follow him in there. But, listen, do not touch anything, understand?"

"Yes, sir," Rand said.

The guard pulled a plastic I.D. card from his pocket, slid it into a slot by the door. It opened.

"Hey," the guard said, his arm extending, "Both of you also

need to leave any electronic equipment out here. Walkie-talkies. Radios. Anything and everything. There are some strange, well, unusual currents in there that could fry them."

Rand remembered Hope's words from The Cavern in Austria. How even a 40-watt light bulb would fry in the presence of the stones.

CHAPTER SIXTY-NINE

The doors closed behind them.

The room was not nearly as immense as the chamber that held the stones in Austria. And the amount of stones were less as well. Only four in this room, but their lack of numbers and size did not diminish their imposing nature, their otherworldly visage. Each stone sat encased on a pedestal, enclosed in the same strange transparent polymer casing.

No lights above, only the hues from the stones. The familiar blues, silver sparkles and a potpourri of dancing cold color on the walls. Rand felt a familiar rush in his bloodstream. An adrenaline surge? The allure? He had to focus. Remember the plan. Disable the guard. Plant the bombs. Leave. Remembered the mantras from his grandfather. Misdirection. Then forced direction. Glanced at his watch. 3:37.

Dropped the clipboard from his hands. It clattered on the floor sending sharp echoes through the room.

"Damn it," he said.

"What's wrong?" Marshall asked.

"Just a damn hand cramp. I get them in this heat out here. Son of a bitch."

He leaned down to pick it up, using his knees instead of his back. Looked up under the brim of his hard hat. Saw the guard's exposed neck. No, not his throat. He didn't want to kill this poor lump. Changed his target to the man's temple. Rand bent his knees more. Placed his hands on the floor in front of him for full balance, much like the linebacker stance he had learned long ago. Short jab. He remembered. Quick. Rhodes' words. Then launched himself at the guard, his right fist extended.

His fist landed on the man's temple and their bodies collided. Rand felt the man's breath escape from his chest. Flattened him to the ground. Rand put his knees on the man's shoulders. Saw the gloves had done their job. The man's temple was red, a deep welt of a bruise already forming, yet Rand's fist felt nothing. No pain. No sting. The guard's eyes fluttered. Half-closed. Open. Closed again. Then unconscious. Knocked out. Rand pulled the Beretta out of the guard's holster, tucked it under his shirt into his waistband. Had nothing to tie the guard up with, except the duct tape in his toolbox. That would do. Turned the man over on his back. Wrapped his hands in duct tape. Rand smiled wryly to himself. He was hoping to blow this place to hell and back and now he was concerned about not killing a man outright. Eliot was right. Our species was weak. Reason anything to our advantage.

CHAPTER SEVENTY

Rand hauled the guard over into a corner, hoping the shadows would conceal him long enough for Rand to do what he had to do and escape. He stood. Surveyed the room again.

"Well, hello old friends," Rand emphasized the nonchalance, hoping to calm his nerves.

Nothing, but the low hum. He remembered that now, too. The hum. And what it meant. All the power. All the access to deepen his knowledge. To enhance his creativity. Here.

Eyed his watch again. 3:43.

Stop. Think, he told himself. Remember the plan. He had four egg timers. He approached the largest piece of the Slendoc Meridian, which was roughly the size of a baseball sitting eye level on the pedestal. Rand gently grabbed each side of the covering and tried to lift it. It wouldn't budge. Shit. Come on. Come on. He didn't want to shoot the covering this time. This was a planned operation. No time for wild abandon like back in Austria. Damn. Damn. He looked around the pedestal for anything. A button. A code box. Anything. Nothing. Then reached under the pedestal. Ran his fingers under it. Felt it. A switch. Heard a lock. Smiled to himself. How simple. Of course there couldn't be a panel or code in here. No electronics. Nothing, but a latch. He gently lifted the cover which was surprisingly light and set it on the floor.

Then he felt it. The draw. The sensory enhancement. The enticement of the stone. All of it resurfaced in Rand. In waves. He inhaled through his nose. Deeply. Closed his eyes. Could feel a tingle in the air. A flutter of electricity traced a haphazard trail down his spine. Opened his eyes. Breathe in. Breathe out. Breathe in.   Breathe out.

Rand shook his head, hoping to shake off the allure. The piercing light sparkled, drew him in like a trance. He could hear the blood rushing in his ears. See the hairs on his arm, raised like a thousand spindly blades of brown grass.

He shook his head again. Focus, damn it. Set his toolbox on the floor. Reached in. Grabbed the egg timer, a hammer and a screwdriver. Set the egg timer carefully beside the stone. The screwdriver and hammer next to it. Eyed his watch. The analog perking along. 3:47. Okay, think. Think. He subtracted. Set the timer for 28 minutes. 4:15 p.m.? Yes. Double checked. Ran the numbers through his head again. Always hated math. 28 minutes. Okay. Good. Rand reached down. Grabbed the covering. Lifted it. Replaced it. Immediately, a breath of relief escaped his lungs. One down. Three to go. He had survived the first test.

CHAPTER
SEVENTY-ONE

Placing the other explosives had been easier. Only one explosive had to be directly by the stone, Eliot had said. The remainder only needed to be in close proximity. Even just in the same room is fine he remembered. He had set the other egg timers on the floor behind the other pedestals, screwdrivers and hammers as companions nestled in the back of the room. Didn't want to chance lifting a covering on another stone. Didn't know if he could withstand the temptation again. Subtracted the time in his head. All set to explode at 4:15.

Rand wiped the sweat from his brow. It was 3:53. He was supposed to meet the group back at the vans in seven minutes. On time, maybe even early. He couldn't believe it.

He began to walk to toward the entrance. Then he felt it. The lure of the stones. Temptation. Perhaps, he could lift the covering on one of them, he told himself. Just to get a hint of the power of the Meridian. Just a quick touch. Only a minute or two. So close. Or he could just steal a sliver. The draw again. He felt his feet walking forward, while his eyes looked around, gazing at every stone. A lust. A craving. A want. A need. He shook his head again. Damn it. Damn it. Why was he even here? Fuck. Doubts edging their way around his mind, regret finding a foothold in his heart. He should've taken the money when he was in Mentone. The new I.D. Gone to South America. He could be drunk on rich, red Chilean wine, dining with gauchos underneath the shadow of mountains. Instead. Here. Now. This again. The temptation, yet the mission. The craving, yet the need for self-discipline. Divorce your mind from passion. Only logic. Strange bastardizations from Dr. Virgillius's sessions echoed back to him. Yes. Yes. It made so much sense now. Maybe even a purpose in remembering that. Divorce your mind from passion.

The doors were only a few yards away. Rand swore he could hear the stones calling his name. So damn entrancing. He began to pick up his pace. Almost run. The doors sighed open. He half-tumbled into the hall.

Startled, the guard turned.

"Whoa, you okay, buddy?"

"Yeah, sorry…that place is weird."

"Yeah, you can say that again. Hey, where's Marshall?"

"Said he needed to see you in there about something. I don't know. My work's done."

"What?" The man said, then turning his head toward the room.

Rand yanked the stolen Beretta from under his shirt and swung it hard at the base of the guard's head. The neck jolted to the side. The body limp, slumped to the floor. Rand hastily wrapped a band of duct tape around the man's hands, tugged a walkie-talkie from the man's pocket.

"Subject knocked unconscious. Threat neutralized," Rand whispered to himself, hoping the stoic vernacular would ward off his encroaching guilt.

Rand eyed the slot for the I.D. card to open the door. Lifted the handgun. Stepped a few feet away. Pulled the trigger. A gunshot. Pulled it again. Another one. Looked at the slot. Damaged. Beyond repair. A jagged hole, smoke rising from a trio of frayed wires sticking their disheveled necks out.

CHAPTER
SEVENTY-TWO

That was as easy as it could have gone, Rand thought. The bombs were planted. He had resisted the lure of the stones. The guards were knocked unconscious. The entrance to the room disabled. The gun in his waistband. The walkie-talkie hooked back on his belt. Ready to go. Looked at his watch. 3:56. He had 4 or so minutes to get to the main floor where the rest of the crew were already waiting, probably packed up and in the van. Cutting it close, but he could make it.

Almost there. Almost there, Rand thought. The elevator loomed ahead. Just a few more steps. The button on the panel lit up. Rand heard the slow rumbling of the elevator descending. Oh shit. Oh shit. Someone was coming down. Rand willed his feet to stay in place, affected a look of boredom, readied a forgetful phrase. Something about the weather. Sports. Anything. He just needed a minute to get in the elevator and leave before they noticed anything. The muted ping of the elevator and the doors slid open.

A man walked out. No fatigues. A lab coat. White. Clean shaven. Aquiline nose. Crew cut. Erusive haughtiness. An iPad in his hand. Behind him, stumbled another figure. A female. Head bent down. Tangled hair fell in front of her face. Behind her, a bulky guard, tight-lipped and beady-eyed.

"How y'all doin'?" Rand said. "Just about quittin' time."

The scientist nodded stoically. The female behind him swiveled her head. Beneath the hair, Rand saw them. Green eyes. Open wide. Mouth half open. A look of shock on a sunken face. It was Hope Lightfoot.

She stopped in her tracks.

The guard behind her bumped into her, a smirk on his face, prodded her in the back with his M16.

"Come on Miss Fancy Feet, keep up, keep up. I'm getting tired of being your babysitter."

She froze. Stared at Rand who stared back. How? How was she here? What was she doing here? He thought she was dead. Gone. Had steeled himself in that resolve and focused on avenging his parents, his grandfather by coming to this place. Taking this action. And now. Alive. In the enemy's lair. And, yet, she looked despondent. A curtain of sad morose hung over her frame. Her arrogance diminished. Any traces of her haughtiness banished. Was she a prisoner? What had happened?

"I said come on, quit staring," the guard poked her again with his weapon. "You've never seen a construction worker before?"

"Ma'am," Rand forced. Raised his hand to tip his hat.

Rand's walkie-talkie beeped.

"I don't mean to sound like an old woman, son, but how about you hustle, we do need to get to the buffet before it closes," Winston said, a lilt to his gruff voice, but also a gentle prod to hurry.

Hope had turned. Her back to him, following the scientist down the hall. Soon they would find the disabled guard. Then the blown card slot. And more. If they had time. Damn. And time was running out. Rand stepped into the elevator. Finger went to punch the button to the top floor. Paused. Knew they were waiting. Ready to go. Hope stopped in the hall. The guard pushed her again. She stumbled. Turned her face to Rand again. A look of confusion. And, above all, fear. What to do? What to do? He glanced at his watch. 3:58. Had to leave. Get as far away as possible. End this madness. Deliver a punch to The Organization. Knock it down. Redemption for his family. The door closed. The panel waiting for him to press a button.

CHAPTER
SEVENTY-THREE

"**D**amn it. Damn it. Damn it," Rand said. Knew what he had to do. Reached under his shirt. Slowly eased the handgun out. Ran his hands over the buttons on his shirt. Tight. Closed. Deep breaths. Pressed the 'Open Door' button on the panel. The soulless ping. The door opened. They were walking down the hall. All of their backs to him. Kill or be killed. Remembered Rhodes' words. He raised the gun, aimed it at the guard's head. Went to squeeze the trigger. Stopped. He could miss. Hit Hope. Damn. No scope on these guns. He didn't trust his aim. Lowered the muzzle of the gun. Pointed the gun at the guard's back. Could he really shoot someone in the back? Kill or be killed. But, he could not shoot someone in the back.

"Hey!" He yelled.

The guard turned around. Surprise on his face.

Rand fired. One round. Two rounds. Three rounds. The man buckled. Red splotches on his chest. Body fell forwards, colliding into the floor, head bouncing off the linoleum. His gun sprawling from his grasp into the corner. Hope turned. Relief and shock in her eyes. The scientist turned. Baffled.

"Duck!" Rand yelled to Hope.

She did not hesitate. Crouched. Rand pointed the gun at the scientist. Squeezed the trigger. The first bullet whizzed by his head.

Crashed into the wall beside him. A spark. Saw the scientist begin to reach inside his coat. For what. A radio? A gun? Rand did not hesitate.

"Stop or I'll shoot. God help me." Enough blood on his hands, damn it. No chances now. No time. "On your knees. Now!"

The scientist withdrew his hand away from his pocket. Knelt. Raised his hands.

"Good. Hope," he said. "Empty his pockets, grab whatever is in there."

He watched her frantically scurry through the man's lab coat. Discovered a walkie-talkie.

"Let's go," Rand said.

She looked at Rand. Then back to the scientist on his knees. Raised her hand in a fist. A swift downward stroke like a lightning bolt. Punched him in the face. He toppled over.

CHAPTER
SEVENTY-FOUR

"**C**ome on!" Rand yelled. He watched as Hope ran to him. Had forgotten her cold brutalness in battle. How she lacked reservation. Half-envied it as she stepped into the elevator. He madly punched the button to the main floor. As the doors closed, he caught a last glimpse of the bloodied face of the scientist staring at them as he lay supine. Infuriation scrawled on his face.

She was breathing heavily. Eyes stared into his. Pleading.

"What are you doing here, I –"

"No time," he said. "Later. Right now, we need to move." He motioned to the walkie-talkie she had pilfered from the scientist. "Turn it on."

Voices came through.

- "Copy that. Some type of noises on the bottom floor. Could be nothing, but it sounded odd. Muffled booms almost. Arrhythmic."

- "Who's down there? Have we contacted them?"

- "I radioed our team down there and no one is picking up. I also tried Doctor McGovern and Fieldstone and am getting nothing from them either. They were taking the girl down there again."

- "Let's send a team down."

- "Yes, chief."

- "I am keeping this line open. I don't like this."

Rand felt like he had heard one of the voices before. A trace of an accent? An inflection? No time to think now. The elevator jostled to a stop.

"Rand, what's the plan? What are you doing here?"

"Shit," Rand said. "Just follow me."

He jammed the gun inside the front of his pants, pulled his shirt over it. The doors opened.

A group of guards were rushing toward them, a rush of sickly olive uniforms.

"Move, move, move," the one in front yelled. "Hold the door."

Rand went to reach for his gun, then realized they had not recognized Hope. Were not coming for him. Wanted the elevator. Rand gently pushed her to the side. She turned, buried her face in his chest.

One of the men bumped into Rand. Turned. Gave him a scowl.

"Sorry man," Rand said.

The man stared at him. A glance at Hope's back. Then the doors closed and the elevator was gone. The atrium empty.

CHAPTER
SEVENTY-FIVE

The vans were waiting under the shadow of the warehouse door, already packed and ready. Small puffs of blue smoke from the tailpipes. Engines purring. Winston's head was leaning out of the driver's side window, a bewildered look on his face as he saw Hope. Rand kept walking. Walk slow, he told himself. Walk slow. He grabbed Hope's hand. She still had her head bent forward staring at the ground. Winston nodded toward the van Rand and Spota had driven in. Rand led Hope to the back. Opened the doors. Pushed Hope in. Half-jogged to the passenger's side. Reached for the handle.

He was hit in the back. Violently. Hard. A sharp needle pain. Then another. Another. It was bullets. Bullets. He heard them now. Gunshots. Saw flashes on the side of the van. Fell to the ground. Turned his body on the floor. Saw a lone man marching toward him, a gun raised. A man about Rand's age. A rage-filled expression on the face. Yet strangely familiar. Eyes the color of screaming blue skies. Flashes jumping from the gun barrel. Then a spark in Rand's face. Eyes shut. Knocked his head against the side of the van. Opened his eyes. Saw now. A bullet had struck his visor. A hairline crack. Another bullet struck his chest. His breath exploded from his lungs. Damn. Damn. Damn. The gunshots stopped. The chamber empty. Rand saw the man shake the magazine loose, it fell to the floor, silently clattering. Rand's ears half deaf from the noise. Saw the man reach toward his pocket for another magazine.

"Get in!" He heard Spota yelling behind him. Rand pushed himself off the floor. Bruised body resisting, pulled himself into the seat, closed the door behind him.

The van sped off, Winston's right in front of them, leading a chaotic escape. Rand looked back. The face stared at his. Eyes met. Who was he?

CHAPTER
SEVENTY-SIX

The vans were barreling manically toward the gate. Rand peered through the window. The domes were blurring by. He knew they had been discovered. Alerted. Something was going to happen. Any minute now. They couldn't get away this easy.

The walkie-talkie burst to life.

"Spota," Winston's voice. "Have you got him?"

"Yes, he's right here."

"Is he okay?"

Rand felt Spota staring at his face.

"I think so, chief…His shirt is beat to hell, but I don't see any blood."

"Let me speak to him."

Rand felt a nudge on his shoulder. Turned. Spota's eyes were on the road following the exhaust trail of Winston's van. His arm was outstretched holding the radio.

Rand grabbed it. Flipped his visor up.

"Yeah," his voice parched. Croaked.

"Rand, what the hell happened back there? Who is that with you?" The voice was angry.

He didn't know what to say. Mind numbed.

"Sorry, Winston. I fucked up. I'm sorry."

He handed the walkie-talkie back to Spota. Shook his head.

Heard Winston speaking but it seemed like a thousand miles away. Confusion washed through his mind.

"Rand? Hello? Rand?"

Spota broke in.

"He's okay, chief. I've got him. Just needs a minute. Let's just get the hell away from here."

Rand peered into the back of the van. Saw Hope huddled against the side. Her arms clutched around her body. Shivering, despite the heat. Her eyes met his.

"You okay?" He asked.

She shook her head yes. No words.

"Hang on," Rand said. "We'll be safe soon."

CHAPTER
SEVENTY-SEVEN

The rocket didn't hit their van, but was just off to the right of the road, its shock bringing Rand back from his daze as earth and fire spewed into the air, tossing black sand and pebbles onto their windshield.

The van half tilted from the blast then plummeted back to the ground, the insides shaking, Rand tossed against his door.

"Damn!" Spota yelled.

"You okay?" Rand asked.

Spota nodded.

"Those bastards have rocket launchers or some shit. Winston better put the pedal to the metal or we're cooked, man."

As if on cue, Winston's van accelerated. The road didn't seem long on the way in, Rand thought. Now, it seemed to stretch forever. And no trees or hills. Exposed. White vans against black sands. Perfect targets. Damn. He looked at the speedometer. It was nearing 90 miles per hour.

"They'll be at the gates waiting for us," Rand said.

"Yep, if they don't blow us to hell first." An emotionless Spota responded.

"Ideas?"

"Fuck no."

"I've got a gun, I was able to, uh, borrow, but I don't know how many rounds are in it."

"Shit, it's better than nothing. Even with these bullet proof vans, it's going to be hell getting out that gate."

The walkie-talkie crackled to life.

Winston's voice. "Son of a bitch. It's going to be hell getting out of here men. Throw out your tools or anything else on the road if you can. Anything to create an obstacle. Hurry!"

"Copy that."

Rand crawled to the back of the van. Opened the door. In the distance, he saw several jeeps pursuing, black sands in a flurry behind them, like demonic chariots leading a sandstorm. He tossed out a toolbox. Two levels. An extra hard hat. Even a fire extinguisher.

"Better than nothing," he said to nobody. Cast a forced smile toward Hope. She didn't return his smile. Slumped.

Rand turned to close the doors. Paused. Waited to see if the obstacles would work. Saw one jeep careen off the road. Another one skid, then spin before rocking to a stop. He couldn't see the other jeeps. Nothing, but a swirl of black sand rising from the ground.

He yanked the doors shut, walked back to his seat and buckled in.

CHAPTER
SEVENTY-EIGHT

The second rocket ripped clean through Winston's van and exploded on the other side of the road. Winston's van slowed, wavered, flames dancing around the gaping hole in its side. Rand watched as it skidded, swerved, almost tipped, then, somehow leveled off, slowed but kept going. Spota gunned the engine, swerved and took the lead.

"Fuck," Spota said. "Fuck. Fuck. We're fucked man, but we've got to give it a shot."

Ahead loomed the guard gate. Less than 100 yards away. Four guards were out there, aiming M-16s, crouched behind the flimsy guardrail.

The van continued to accelerate. 100, 110, 120 miles per hour.

"Shit," Spota said, "We might have a chance. Time to use that gun. Pull that sucker out and empty it on those bastards."

"You know the chances of me hitting them in transit are about 1,000 to –"

"I don't care!" The first time Rand ever heard him raise his voice. "I don't care. Just aim and fire. Do it. We need it. We need anything."

Rand rolled down the window, tried to steady the gun. Thought he had a decent aim. Began firing, emptying the last 7 or 8 shots. Could not tell if they hit anything. The guards did not budge. Then flashes from their guns. A raining of shots hit their windshield, like a pelt of hail from an angry sky. Another blitz of bullets punching the hood. Bullets pinging off everywhere. The gate ahead. Just yards now. Spota gave the engine a final push and they broke through the gate, glancing one of the guards. The others diving out of the way. A rough bump, then they were on the road, pushing ahead, Black Sands finally behind them.

Spota plucked the walkie-talkie off the floor.

"Winston? You there? You with us? Over."

Just a hiss.

"Damn," Spota said. "I can't see out of these mirrors. Are they back there? What the hell is going on?"

Rand tried to peer in the rear view mirror, could see nothing through the dirt-splattered window. Rolled it down. Stuck his head out, the wind ripping a torrent by him.

Winston's van was still behind them, but was slowing, then crawling to a stop.

"Stop!" Rand said. "Stop! They're there. But, something is wrong."

"Rand," he said. "We don't have time. They are going to be out here any second scouring these mountains to find us. The bombs are going to go off soon. We've got to get to our rendezvous point and get away as far as possible."

Rand looked at his watch. 4:06.

"Just a minute. Let me go check on them. Throw it in reverse. Just one minute!"

"Fuck. Okay, we're out of range of the rocket launchers. But just one minute!"

Spota pulled over onto the shoulder of the road. A look of agitation on his face.

"Damn it. One minute. That's it."

CHAPTER
SEVENTY-NINE

Winston was still in the driver's seat, but how he was still steering was beyond Rand's guess.

The right side of his face was matted with blood. His right eye shut. Blood on the seat, dozens of small bits of metal embedded in his shirt and his exposed neck. His body was rigid, but he was alive. Rhodes was better, but was in shock, maybe concussed. His eyes glazed. Silent.

"Come on," Rand said to Winston. "Let's go. Rhodes can you make it on your own?"

A dazed nod.

"Good, I'll get Winston then. Let's hurry."

He reached down to Winston's seatbelt, the silver buckle stained with blood, the strap singed. Winston draped an arm over Rand's shoulder.

"Come on, come on. Just a few steps to our van and we'll be fine. Just a few steps."

Winston limped forward. His hard hat tumbled onto the asphalt. Rand half-carried him to the van, lifted him through the doors into the back, tried to lay him gently.

"Get something on his cuts. Uh, pressure. Stop the bleeding. Give him water. I don't know. Do something. Anything," he told Hope, making it up as he went along. He had no idea what to do or what to say. Rhodes behind him now. Swaying. Climbed in.

"What happened?" Rhodes asked. "Where are we?"

"Uh, I'll explain later. Just get in. Just get in. We need to go."

Then almost on cue. He heard it.

A bastardized symphony that stirred his stomach.

A faint siren.

The sound of approaching cars and beyond it, the unnatural deep whir of a helicopter's blades slicing through the air.

CHAPTER EIGHTY

Rand slammed the doors shut. Ran to the passenger's seat, climbed in and Spota peeled out.

"What's the story Rand?"

"Uh, bad. Winston is a mess. Rhodes is in shock. Doesn't know where the hell he is."

"That's great. Shit. Just me and you."

"Yeah."

"Any sign of pursuit."

Rand hesitated.

"Ah, I didn't see anything, but I heard them. More jeeps I bet. Sirens. And a helicopter."

"Damn. A helicopter?"

"Yeah."

Spota flipped his wrist. Eyed his watch.

"Okay, we've got about six minutes until that place blows if they haven't found the treats we left them. We're about half a mile from our spot. We still got a chance."

"Yeah?"

"Hell, yeah," a glimmer of optimism in the voice. "If we can get to the Humvee, we have a shot. Heavy armor, speed, weapons and if that bitch goes up in flames, there will be enough of a distraction to help us out."

Rand nodded.

"Hold on, here we go."

Spota swerved onto a barely perceptible dirt road that ran into a thicket of Ponderosa pine. The van swerved through a forsaken logging road and stopped in a clearing.

"We're here."

"What?"

"There it is."

Rand could see nothing. Had Spota been knocked crazy too? He squinted. Then he saw it. The faint outline of a sheet. Odd reflections. That was it then. They had not lied. It blended in perfectly.

"Damn, too bad we can't drive it with that sheet on."

"Yeah, right? But it still has some tricks. Come on. Let's go."

CHAPTER EIGHTY-ONE

The Humvee sat eight and also had the ability to fold down seats for what was close to bedding. They gingerly slid Winston in. Laid him down. One eye still open. Fluttering. Mouth muttering indistinctly. Hope slid in beside him, their hands clasped.

Spota in the driver's seat, yelling back to Hope.

"There's medical supplies back there. Just open the compartments. There's also guns. Pass them up."

Rand went to help Rhodes, who was still sitting in the van. Took his hand guided him through the double doors.

"Let's go."

Rhodes clamored out slowly. Stood staring blankly toward the sun.

"Let's go," Rand said.

Rhodes didn't budge. Stood staring blankly at the sun.

"Come on, we –"

Rand didn't finish his sentence as a black helicopter swept over the tops of the trees, banked and then wheeled back. Rand went to grab Rhodes' hand. A chatter of machine guns from above. Limbs splitting like thunder, the sound of a thousand chops. The staccato rhythm the gun intermingled with the cracks of wood splitting as limbs and leaves rained down on them, their fertile bark splintered into wood shards.

"Come on!" Rand yelled, tugging at Rhodes' arm, who still stood transfixed. The ground exploded around them. Bullets raining into the earth. Rand felt one smash into his arm, began to pull away from Rhodes. Rhodes turned to him. The same glassy look in his eyes. Then silence. A horn. A yell.

"Get in!" Spota yelling. "They're reloading and coming back. You have to get in now."

Rand yanked Rhodes arm. Hard. He stumbled toward the vehicle, clumsily climbed in. Rand could see nothing in his eyes. The man was numb.

CHAPTER
EIGHTY-TWO

The Humvee barreled out of the clearing, climbing up a small rise through the traces of the road. A muffled boom. "And that would be the van," Spota said. "Let's hope we won't be next."

He punched in several buttons on a console on the dashboard. Turned around.

"You got those guns?"

"Yes," Hope's voice small.

Two Uzis were handed up. Rand turned, grabbed them. Spota began giving orders.

"Check em. There should also be a Grand Power handgun under your seat?"

"Yeah," Rand said.

"Okay, good," Spota said, then half-turning. "What's going on back there? How's Winston? Is he stabilized?"

"He's...Okay," Hope answered. "I can't find where the bleeding is coming from. I patched a cut over his eye. His chest looks fine, the shirt stopped most of the shrapnel. He's got an IV running, but his blood pressure is low. I can't find where the bleeding is coming from."

"Okay, keep checking. Check his back. That missile went through the van like a bat out of hell. Some shrapnel or something might have come up through his seat. Turn him over, but do it slowly if you can."

"Yes."

Rand turned. Hope focused on Winston. The one eye half-open. Mouthed something. Damn, Rand thought. Damn. I fucked up. Damn. Breathe. Breathe, he told himself.

"Highway ahead," Spota said. "Hold on."

The vehicle roared out of the woods and bounced onto the highway. A skid, then straightened.

"Well, that was good," Spota said. "Great balance, now let's see what this engine can do."

CHAPTER EIGHTY-THREE

The vehicle was clipping along at 100 miles per hour, hugging the road as it wound through the mountains. Rand felt like he was on a roller coaster unleashed to its own volition. No traffic. Rand had heard the faint chop of the helicopter a few times, but they had not been detected. The radar on the dashboard showed it off to the west near where they had ditched the van. The side mirror revealed nothing but asphalt. Ahead, a vacant highway.

Rand wanted a cigarette. Fidgeted in his seat. Checked his watch. Any minute now. If it was going to happen.

"How are we? On distance? Are we far enough away?" Rand asked.

Spota glanced at the console, eyed the digital map. The shape of a car blinking along the road.

"Close. Real close. Just getting ready to clear this ridge to give us some cover. Any minute now, right?"

"Yeah…if it happens."

"Hey Rand, who is she? What the fuck happened back there? Everything was on schedule on our end. You were a couple of minutes late. And then – I mean – what the hell happened? You show up with this girl, that man comes running out with a gun firing like crazy at us and all hell breaks loose."

"Shit, I know." Rand looked to the window. Edges of guilt now.

Did he do the right thing? And, if so, at what cost? What about Winston? What about the mission? Everything. "She's with me, she's one of us, she –"

A groan from the back. Winston coughed. Hope had rolled him onto the side. Rand craned his neck to the back and saw the entrance wound. A chunk of twisted metal the size of a hand was embedded in the man's back. A nasty twisted piece, like a jagged knife serrated his back. The blood wasn't pouring out, but the wound was gruesome.

Hope looked at Rand.

"If we take it out, he will die. It is the only thing right now keeping, keeping him together. Keeping the artery pinched."

"And, if we leave it in?"

"Yes, he will die."

"Damn it. I knew you were going to say that. Fucking Catch 22."

"We need to find a medical facility, we need –"

CHAPTER EIGHTY-FOUR

The sky went white. Then flashed back to blue.

The lights on the console began blinking, then shut down. Faint red emergency lights shot out of corners in the vehicle as it rolled to a stop.

A thump in the distance. Then a few more. Like the sound of fireworks being shot off.

"Hold on for the bump," Spota said.

"Bump?"

"The shock wave."

Rand heard the wind before he felt it. A deep howl. Then a push of earth, sand, trees, grit swept over them. The air around the truck swirling black and brown. Then a thump. Deep. Deep delving thump. The car was lifted into the air. Levitated for a moment. Suspended. Rand lifted his arms out as if wanting to brace himself. Then the Humvee dropped. The air began to clear. The road covered in sand and twigs.

"It worked. Damn, it worked," Rand whispered, almost reverently.

"Yeah," Spota said, then a glimpse of the cocky smile crossed his face. "Of course it did. I told you it would."

Spota punched a button on the dashboard. Held it for a minute. Rand heard a switch click. The red lights shut off, the console woke up, lights blinking and the motor hummed to life.

Spota blew out a long sigh.

"Now, let's get out of here."

CHAPTER
EIGHTY-FIVE

"How far to the safe house?" Rand asked.

"We got about 2 more hours. Should be crossing the border in about 20 minutes."

"Stupid question at the 11th hour, but how are we going to get this thing, this huge machine and us across the border? I mean, Winston is hurt, Hope doesn't even have a passport."

"We pay them. The guy at our crossing, local authorities, everything. We're clean. Good to go. Been using these guys for years. Keep your gun handy just in case, but I'm not expecting any issues. We've worked with this group for a long time. So, yeah, we pay them off. Slip over. We'll be in our house in an area named Rancho San Fernando drinking beer before you know it."

CHAPTER
EIGHTY-SIX

There was the faintest glow of a red circle in the distance that swayed back and forth, like a buoy in a sea. Rand squinted through the dimmed headlights, but couldn't decipher what it was.

"Spota, do you see a red dot ahead or am I going crazy?"

"No, you aren't crazy. That is our spot. Our destination. On a clear night in the desert you can see a mile away. That must be Florence. She is a wonderful physician and fastidious, too. We will soon be in good hands, my friend."

They had crossed the U.S.-Mexico border an hour and a half ago. As Spota had promised, it went smoothly and quickly. As they sped through a moonless Mexican night, Rand had tried to distract himself by keeping a keen eye on the rear view mirror, but Winston's groans and the disheveled Hope consumed his thoughts. He tried not to stare into the back of the Humvee too much, but couldn't help himself. Winston, occasional coughs, peppered with blood. Hope over him, wiping his brow, whispering low tones that conveyed comforting words. And then Rhodes staring vacantly at the side of the vehicle.

Guilt nagged at his conscience, shades of remorse tugged at his heart. The mission a success, yet Winston lay dying, Rhodes was in a state somewhere beyond reach. And for what? For a woman. But, not any woman. Hope Lightfoot. A woman he loved. A woman important for her work, too, he reasoned. Then he tried to stop his mind. He could argue the merits of both sides back and forth until he was too tangled up to do anyone any good.

"Hey," Spota leaned over whispering, breaking Rand's silent battle. "You never told me. The details. Who is she? You know her, right? I can see that much, but who is she and how did you find her?"

Rand tensed. Felt the tease of a tear in his eye. The slight burn of salt.

"She's," his throat caught, "She's Hope...Hope Lightfoot...She helped me destroy what they were doing in Austria...she's also," the word, 'girlfriend' flet through his mind, but it sounded too flighty, "She's...my lady...I thought she was dead. But, found her...inside..of there. I'm sorry, I just, I just couldn't let her stay there."

He coughed. Pushing the tears back. Cleared his throat.

"Does that make sense?" He asked.

"Yeah, it does. That's crazy...I thought, we had heard she was dead or missing or whatever when they raided Mentone."

"That's what I thought too. I don't know what happened or how she got there. There hasn't been a lot of time to discuss, you know?"

Spota wryly smiled.

"Yeah, I know. Don't worry, my friend, we'll be at the safe house before you know it, then we can all have a good shower, drink a few dozen beers and tell each other our stories."

Rand glanced into the back seat. Winston seemed to be teetering on the edge of consciousness. There would be no beer for him, Rand thought. Damn.

CHAPTER
EIGHTY-SEVEN

Rand could see barbed wire fences baring broken brown teeth in the dull headlights. A long dirt road. Then the house itself. Not regal, but welcoming. No rickety wooden boards to clatter, but a simple Adobe brick.

Florence, a stocky woman in her early 50s, met them in front of the house, her red-eyed lantern dangling from her hand. An accent born out of the Scotland Highlands.

"Welcome boys. I've been waiting for you all night. I've got some dinner on the stove, you can park the Humvee in the barn out back, also –"

"Ms. Florence," Spota interrupted, "we've got a sick man in here who needs help. We've got to get him in the house and in the medical quarters as soon as possible."

"Oh, dear me, I'm sorry. Yes, of course."

She turned back to the house, gave a short whistle. Two men Rand had not noticed before emerged from the shadows. Clad in all black fatigues. Modified M249 Light Machine Guns slung across their backs. God knows what else concealed on their persons, Rand thought.

"We need a stretcher and an IV unit too," Florence shouted, "Bring out Dr. Jabren now."

One of the men ran inside the house, the other strode to the Humvee.

"What can I do ma'am?" He asked.

"Anyone else, hurt?" She asked Spota.

"I don't know how bad, but, yeah, we've got two more in the back that need to be checked out. Probably just a concussion and shock, but it can't hurt."

"Okay," she said, then turning to the man, "Help the other two in and then come back if we need you for the stretcher."

"Yes ma'am."

CHAPTER
EIGHTY-EIGHT

Rand tilted an ice cold bottle of Modelo to his mouth, relishing the cold liquid, hoping the beer would quell his anxiety. Him and Spota both sitting on a worn couch in what Rand assumed was the den of the house. They both needed showers and "a quick look over from the doctor" as Florence had insisted, but both declined. Were waiting to see what the diagnosis was on Winston. No nervous small talk now. A resigned quietness between them.

"You want another beer?" Spota asked.

"Yeah, sure," Rand said. "Thanks."

"Of course, I told you we'd be drinking beer in a couple of hours." A faint smile. Rand could not comprehend how this man kept up such a positive attitude, even in the direst of circumstances.

Before he could fetch a drink, Florence appeared at a door.

"Boys, you need to come down now." An urgency in her voice.

Neither of them said anything, but followed her down a dimly lit wood-paneled hall to a staircase. Descending, Rand caught the waft of antiseptic and latex. At the bottom of the staircase was an operating theater. The three of them peered through a large window. Winston lay on a hospital bed, his face frosty pale barely visible above a white surgical blanket. An IV and a blood bag both hung on a stand, their lines snaking underneath the gown.

A lone doctor stood beside him clad in the ugly green gowns of hospitals and funereal white gloves. He glanced up. Saw Spota and Rand and walked out to greet them.

"Gentlemen, I'm Doctor Jabren." The voice deep, but clinical. "Winston is in very bad shape. To put it simply, his spine was punctured by a projectile which severed a main artery. The blood loss has been steady, but due to the odd placement of the shrapnel, it has also been slow with the projectile acting almost as a cauterizer without getting too technical. However – "

"Is he going to okay?" Rand interrupted.

The doctor stared at him.

"Frankly, no. The outlook is dire. I can try to fix him, but the percentages are against us. I talked with him about it – the surgery, effects afterwards such as partial paralysis, the recovery time and so on, but he said he is 'ready to go home' as he put it. He has requested a strong morphine drip and for me to remove the object. He did request to talk to you both, separately, before I begin the procedure. I imagine this is difficult, but you need to see him immediately."

Rand was silent. Knew it was coming. But, still, the words of it. The finality did not make the situation better.

"Okay," Spota said. "I'll go in there. Do I need to scrub up or put on a mask?"

The doctor tightened his lips.

"No, it doesn't matter anymore."

CHAPTER
EIGHTY-NINE

Rand felt like he was watching television on mute. Could not hear the words. Only see. The occasional tear dripping down Spota's cheek. The ghost of a smile on Winston's face. Could almost guess what they were saying. Spota cracking a joke. Winston retorting. Rand stared down at his boots. Fine dust covering the shoelaces, stuck in the eyelets, sprinkled across the toe. Looked up. At the doctor. At Florence. Tried to distract himself. Could think of nothing to say. No wit or jokes or observations. The three of them just witnesses to a sad ritual. A movement caught his eye. His eyes back to the window. Saw Spota grip Winston's shoulder. More words. Then a final nod. Back through the door. Met Rand. Sniffling.

"All right, my friend, your turn."

Rand planted a hand on Spota's shoulder, then hugged him. Felt the man's body shaking under him, the silent convulsions of grief.

"Okay, okay," Spota coughed. "Get in there. Your turn."

Rand left the embrace, walked through the door. To the bed.

Winston's face was washed out, a faint sheen darker than the sheet above him. The wrinkles in his face now like tiny rivers, the whiskers more white than black, like frost bitten branches. A bandage over one eye. His hair matted and streaked with blood.

"Hey son, how you doin'?" He whispered.

"Fine, just fine," Rand replied mechanically, the words robotically tumbling from his mouth.

Winston coughed, then, "That's good, because you look like shit."

Rand coughed a small laugh, the salt of tears wrestling with it in his throat. Winston gave a weak smile.

"Damn Winston, I'm sorry. I'm so, so sorry. I fucked up everything." The lump in Rand's throat swelling.

"No, no, no. You did great...we," a cough. "We hit those bastards good didn't we? Spota said everything worked."

"Yeah, but, but, you. I'm sorry, we could have gotten away, but I saw Hope and – "

"Ssshhhh," Winston whispered, almost maternally. "Stop that... she took good care of me on the ride down here....gentle touch... sweet voice...that's the girl you were talking about when we first met."

Rand nodded. A faint smile from Winston returned.

"It's okay Rand. She's a keeper. I can't see worth a shit with only one eye, but she's a looker, too."

The tears came freely now. Rand used the back of his sleeve to wipe them from his cheek. Tried to speak. Couldn't. The tears too much.

"Ssshhh," Winston said, "that's enough. Cry for me when I'm gone, but not now, you're just depressing me."

Rand gave another sorrowful laugh, choked with tears. Winston's good eye was half-shut now. The wrinkles on his face relaxing.

"Listen, son. You did good. Don't blame yourself for anything. We had a snowball's chance in hell of pulling that off, especially with all the last-minute improvising. It was a fool's errand. Hell, I never expected to even make it this far alive...you did good. Never forget that."

"Yes, sir," Rand said, his voice shaky, riddled with emotion.

"One more thing." A cough.

"Yes, sir."

"Your parents would've been damn proud of you. Your grandfather, too." A barrage of coughs. "I'm proud of you. And this is good. This is right. I needed one more rodeo. It's a helluva way to go out. Better than alone in my house watching TV."

"Yes, sir."

"Here, take my hand."

Rand reached below the cool sheets. Felt the calloused palm. Squeezed it gently. There was no return motion.

No words between them now. Winston's breathing shallow. Was he asleep?

Another cough.

"Son, I think it's about time for me to go across that river…I'll tell your daddy and momma hello…tell them what a good man you are," another fit of coughing. "Yep, it's time for me to go across that river." A shiver ran through the body. "I can see my Lucy now. Let's rest under the cool shade of the trees."

CHAPTER
NINETY

A blazing cloudless afternoon, amplified by the glittering azure of the ocean. It was the middle of September and most of the tourists had left, only a few stragglers here and there, the very young and the very old. A beach ball rolled down the sand, specks of sand glinting in the sun. Rand sipped on a Modelo, feet buried in the sand and looked up and down the coast. Had not been able to relax enough to close his eyes and lean on the recliner, so, instead, he sat up and watched the world around him. A few yards away a red kite danced in the air. The gentle lull of the waves.

They had been at a small town in the Baja Pacific Sur for two weeks. Rhodes had joined them for a few days then left for Amsterdam, his talk riddled with allusions to European women and the need to unplug his mind for a few weeks. They had a somber celebratory farewell, which even Rhodes' purchase of Dom Perignon could not elevate.

Rand had barely left their hotel room the first few days. He stayed in a chair by the bed where Hope lay. She had barely moved since they arrived. Laid in bed most of the day. Was unusually quiet. Half sleeping. Half staring. Rand did not know what had happened to her, but she wasn't the same person anymore. Had been transformed somehow. She smiled sometimes. She never shunned him. But, their words were few and Rand learned not to pepper her with questions. So, he brought her meals and devoted the time in their room to sipping coffee and slipping outside for the occasional cigarette. Wanting to do something. Anything. Instead, a feeling of impotence in the face of adversity. A surge of restlessness. And anger.

Spota had convinced him to join him on the beach, saying, "when she's ready, she'll talk, but it isn't helping either of you by you sitting with her all the time. She might just need space and by looking at you, you need some sun." Rand had taken him up on his advice three days before and the situation seemed primed for a turn. Hope had even agreed to join him for dinner that night. Their first night out since they arrived. Their first date. Ever.

He promised not to drink too much before dinner, but she said she didn't care if he did. "Go. Enjoy your afternoon. You need it." He hadn't argued.

Now, he was relishing another day of the Pacific sun. Dug his feet further in the sand, the warm embrace of the beach. Spota sat beside him on a beach recliner, a Dutch woman by him, a tiny lace of bikini over supple skin, rubbed sunscreen on his back. Giggling at his quiet jokes he whispered in her ear.

Rand smiled.

The symphony of the ocean at his feet. The rhythm of the waves flowing and ebbing. Boom. Crash. Boom.

A man in a white suit and white hat was walking near the coastline, urging himself forward with a black cane. The sound of children's laughter from somewhere. Rand sipped on the beer, his hand slippery with the condensation. A strong breeze, the salt tang. A pair of bikini clad women running toward the water, svelte flesh, lust-craving in the light. The red kite danced wildly. The sun on his skin. The man in the white hat looked at Rand. Smiled.

THE APPENDICES

Compiled by Thomas J. Callahan

While we may not know the author's intent in this book, the allusions, philology and symbology are too significant to write off as chance or coincidence. Thus, as with his other works, I have taken the time to examine some of the meaning and intent behind certain names and places in this book with the hope of adding a sliver of illumination. The majority of topics, people and places covered in "Alexandria Rising" are omitted from these appendices or abbreviated in length and detail. For more comprehensive information, I recommend visiting the website, www.alexandriarising.com and reading The Appendices of, "Alexandria Rising."

Mentone, Ala.: Mentone is a small town in northwest Alabama that sits at roughly 1,737 feet above sea level. The area surrounding Mentone is a lush, unspoiled area that includes such sights as Little River Canyon, DeSoto Falls and Lookout Mountain. The town itself is gorgeous and features an eclectic variety of restaurants and shops.

Dr. Dunkel: Dunkel is the German word for 'dark.' Dunkel was Virgillius's assistant in "Alexandria Rising." He had been with The Organization for over 20 years before defecting. His background and education is unknown.

The Castle: Little is known of The Castle where The Organization housed their European headquarters. It was located in the northern part of Austria, possibly within or near the Kalkapen

National Park before it was destroyed by Rand O'Neal during the events of, "Alexandria Rising."

Declan Gola: Declan Gola is from Phoenix, Arizona and spent one year at California Technical University working for a variety of start-ups in the San Francisco bay area where he was recruited to help with communications and IT work at the Mentone outpost. It is worth nothing that Gola is an anagram of Iago, the famous traitor who sets up and betrays Othello in the play of the same name. It would make sense since as another tie-in to Shakespeare and his work which play a strong role in "Alexandria Rising." *"Men should be what they seem," – Othello.*

Presque Isle, ME: Presque Isle is the largest city in Aroostook County, Maine. The population was 9,171 in 2015 as estimated by the U.S. Census. The city is home to the University of Maine at Presque Isle, Northern Maine Community College, Husson University Presque Isle.

Winston Worsley: Winston was a key code breaker and cipher creator for The Organization and Those Who Split for many decades. As he told Rand, he was raised in Texas. Winston spent the bulk of his time with The Organization in Europe working behind-the-scenes. While in London, he met and married Lucy Galmish. His name has caused puzzlement among some researchers and readers. While Winston may appear to allude to historical characters, none of them appear to fit the mold. More importantly is noting his last name. Worsley appears to be a direct reference to Frank Worsley who was the esteemed captain of *The Endurance*, the ship of the miraculous Antarctican mission led by Sir Ernest Shackleton in the early 20th century.

Andrew O'Neal: Finally, we are revealed some insights into Rand's parentage. Andrew O'Neal, nameless in "Alexandria Rising," was the son of Henry O'Neal. He was a highly-regarded operative for The Organization, until he led The Split. Andrew was educated at Berry College and The University of Chicago.

He often served as an adjunct lecturer in between jobs at colleges throughout the Southeast until his murder ordered by Kent St. James.

Madeline Lehmann O'Neal: Andrew O'Neal's wife. She was born in Washington, D.C., educated at Washington & Lee and The University of Chicago where she met Andrew. The entire breadth of her work is unknown as of this writing, however, she is considered by many to be an unsung force in The Split. Described by many as, "only her gracefulness surpasses her intelligence."

Lux Engineering: Lux, i.e., Latin for "light" engineering was, as Winston said, founded in the 1970s.

Harding County, NM: This county has a population of roughly 700. Its geography is a mix of prairie, semi-desert and canyons and is considered to be one of the best kept secrets of natural beauty in that state.

Mary Celest: Little is known of her prior to her work with The Organization. Some have speculated she was raised in the Pacific Northwest, other records point to Morocco. We know she worked with Winston for years in The European Sector primarily in Berlin and London. Interestingly enough, the name, 'Mary Celest' also appears to be tied to the ship Mary Celeste. This mysterious ship was found abandoned and adrift in the Atlantic Ocean in the 1870s and is a source of mystery even today.

Eliot Waterstone: This enigmatic leader is by many estimates 120 years old. According to the "Lost Letters of Henry O'Neal," a supplementary second appendices to "Alexandria Rising," Waterstone recruited Rand's grandfather Henry in the 1940s. Waterstone is also alluded to on various "Alexandria Rising" related websites and discovered videos. Eliot, as he prefers to be called, cites several direct passages from T.S. Eliot during his conversations with Rand O'Neal suggesting a deeper understanding or grasp of things around him. The direct use of passages from T.S. Eliot has been proven as an intentional homage by the author. Eliot has been known by many other names throughout the years including, 'The Kestrel' and 'The Elegant Executioner.' I am laboring deeply to discover more on this man who appears to be - as his name suggests - the key operative of much we cannot see.

Spota: Adam 'Spota' Tiskinski rose through the ranks of the Miami public school system in an odd parallel of academic prowess and a rash of disciplinary issues. Despite being dismissed from three public schools, he still earned a scholarship to MIT. Records of him from that point appear disjointed, but his name does crop up in relation to work with the U.S. Special Forces and as an adjunct professor at Cornell University.

John Reuel Rhodes: Allegedly from Oakland, Rhodes enlisted in the U.S. Marines where he earned accolades for his hand-to-hand combat skills. On-record mission work include missions in Somalia and Iraq before receiving an honorable discharge. He has many aliases including, Jon Wallace and Ron Jones. Curiously, his middle name resembles that of author J.R.R. Tolkien though no direct line of relation has been established, yet.

Black Sands: On paper, an environmental research facility location inside the Gila National Forest in New Mexico. The strange black sands for which it is named are an anomaly to that region, however, the geology aids in their alleged biological experiments.

Ian: Apparently in charge of The Organization's North American headquarters. No last name is given. All reports only cite a young man in his late 20s/early 30s who is, "reckless, ruthless and relentless."

About the Author

Mark Wallace Maguire is the author of the novel, *"Alexandria Rising: Book 1 of The Alexandria Rising Chronicles,"* and *Letters from Red Clay Country: Selected Columns"* a non-fiction work that features the best of his award-winning newspaper and magazine columns. He has been honored by organizations including The Associated Press, The Society of Professional Journalists and The Georgia Poetry Society. In 2005, he was named the Berry College Outstanding Young Alumni of The Year.

You can learn more about him at www.markwallacemaguire. com

Made in the USA
Columbia, SC
07 August 2017